AR Quiz # 114911
BL 3.0   3pts

W9-BAS-346

Jack and Rebel,
the Police Dog

ALSO AVAILABLE:

I, JACK

Jack and Rebel, the Police Dog

by Jack the Dog

as told to
Patricia Finney

illustrated by
Peter Bailey

■ HarperCollins*Publishers*

Jack and Rebel, the Police Dog
Text copyright © 2002 by Patricia Finney
Illustrations copyright © 2002 by Peter Bailey
A paperback edition of this book was published in the United Kingdom
in 2002 by Corgi Yearling Books.
Library of Congress Cataloging-in-Publication Data
Finney, Patricia, date.
Jack and Rebel, the police dog / by Jack the dog, as told to Patricia
Finney ; illustrated by Peter Bailey. —1st U.S. ed.
p. cm.
Summary: Jack the dog returns to tell a tale of his adventures with his
new friend Rebel, a police dog.
ISBN-13: 978-0-06-088049-1 (trade bdg.)
ISBN-10: 0-06-088049-X (trade bdg.)
ISBN-13: 978-0-06-088050-7 (lib. bdg.)
ISBN-10: 0-06-088050-3 (lib. bdg.)
I. Bailey, Peter, date., ill II. Title.
2006036322
CIP
AC

1 2 3 4 5 6 7 8 9 10
❖
First U.S. edition, 2007

To my walkies leash!!! YIPPEE!

CONTENTS

1   Hi There, Friend!   1

2   *VROOM!* Also, CHIPS!   4

3   Garage Dog! GRRRRR   9

4   I DRIVE A CAR   15

5   OH NO! HELP!   18

6   OH WOW! SMELL! IT'S REBEL!   24

7   EEEEOOOOO **MONSTER!**   27

8   Whew!   30

9   My Pack Comes Back   33

10   We Find a Mature BONE!   40

11   Welcome, New Packmembers!   45

12   Flying Feathery!   50

13   Oh NO! BAD Carry-boxes!   57

14   BACON SANDWICH! ❤ ❤ ❤   63

15   REBEL! Again!   66

16   Soft Apedog Dens; Ape-puppies   71

17   BURGER WRAPPERS!
     BAKED BEANS!   77

18   Caroline Comes to Our Den   84

19   NEENAW! NEENAW!   89

20   How Funny!   96

21   Oh Dear. Scary Fierce
     Male Apedogs   111

22   Oh NO! Stranger!   121

23   Hunting with Rebel!   129

24   Rabbits?   139

25   DOUGHNUT! FOR ME! ♥ 154

26   DIG! DIG!   159

27   I GET STEAK!   175

     Jackspeak: English   185

INTERPRETER'S NOTE

Speaking as Jack's real Pack Lady and interpreter, I would like to make certain things clear.

First, although most of the animals are real, ALL OF THE PEOPLE ARE INVENTED AND SO IS THE STORY ITSELF.

There is no such place as South Cornwall, nobody is trying to build a highway through it, and there are no such people as the Stopes family— although there may be accidental resemblances to some of Jack's Packmembers. I'm afraid the Pack Lady in the story is a lot smaller, slimmer, and more patient than me.

Jack is a Real Dog and has certainly helped me with this book, by clumsying all the computer cables and eating my snail mail.

The Cats are real and just as superior: their full names are Remillard (Remy), Amazon (Maisie), and Musketeer (Muskie).

Police Dog Rebel is named after a real police dog that Jack's real Packleader met in the course of his work. Two of the incidents mentioned about him actually happened, although the original Rebel has probably retired by now. I would like to thank PC

Dave Bulley and the Police Dog Unit in Cornwall for their kind help in explaining what police dogs do and how they do it, and if I have made mistakes when I write about PD Rebel and his (fictional) Packleader, I hope they'll let me off this time. Also I'd like to make it clear that Police Dog Rebel is a made-up character, and the police dogs I met while I was researching the book are proper working dogs who would never be such wallies.

Thanks to my test readers—the real Caroline Burley, Martin Fenton, and my daughter, Alex. If I've forgotten anyone, thanks and please forgive me.

Patricia Finney

Jack and Rebel,
the Police Dog

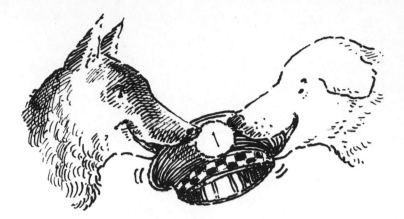

Hi There, Friend!

Hi! HI THERE! HI FRIEND, HOW LOVELY TO SMELL YOUR FRIENDLY SMELL AGAIN, HI HI HI!
HAPPY DOG, HAPPY! HAPPY!

AROOOOF. I remember you! Can I smell your . . . ?

Oh. Sorry.

I am JACK, old-fashioned yellow Labrador who is Very Thick. I have a Great Big apedog Packleader called Tom Stopes and also Dad, and a Fierce apedog Pack Lady called Charlotte and also Mom, and I have three ape-puppies called Terri and Pete and Mikey. Apedogs are funny. They stand on their back legs and they have no tails. (POOR POOR APEDOGS, I will lick it better. . . . Oh, sorry).

I love everyone in my apedog Pack. Almost as much as STEAK.

Then there are the dog-puppies who happened to my Junior Pack Lady, Petra. Everything is different now. Petra's Pack Lady went away, the one who didn't like dogs, so Petra and her puppies went to live with her apedog Packleader next door. I am a bit Sad Dog because it was nice being with Petra, but a bit Not-too-sad Dog because the puppies kept chewing my ears and my tail. We all go for Walkies sometimes as a Big Pack.

My Pack is bigger than your Pack, look!

Oh. Okay.

(Also we have funny-looking normal-walking dogs[1] with hidden claws. They tell me things.)

This story is about me and my friend Police Dog Rebel. He is a Big Fierce Dog, lots of dark fur, big teeth, pointy ears, big swooshy tail. Well, he is a bit fierce. Fiercer than me, anyway.

BUT we are FRIENDS (SO WATCH OUT, GARAGE DOG, ONE DAY WE WILL COME AND MAKE YOU INTO MEAT. . . . GRRRR).

Also it is about me and a Car.

And a rabbit hole.

And nice tasty mature bones.

---

[1] Unfortunately the Big Yellow Stupid is still too thick to realize that, actually, we are Cats. To be precise: Very Large Striped He Who Owns the Radiator, known to the apecats as Remy; Smaller but Fierce Black with a Bit of White She Who Owns the Sofa, known to the apecats as Maisie; and Large but Dim White with Black Spots Who Can Have a Small Armchair if He's Good, known to the apecats as Muskie. Could we get on with the story now, please?

VROOM! Also, CHIPS!

A Car is a big kennel made of metal. It has paws, and it can move, but the paws turn into round things when it stops. It has a short tail that makes horrible whooshy-head smells and smoke. My Packleader's car makes lots of smoke. Lots and lots. More than yours.

Apedogs get in the car to go on the Big Hunt. I can go in the car too. I am not like the Cats. I do not go *Awwooooo, yow, gurrroooomiaaaaaaooooowwwww* like the Cats when I am in the car.[1]

Here we are! It's time to go in the car and do

---

[1] This wicked libel is the Big Yellow Stupid's misunderstanding of our dignified and restrained protests when put in a horrible barred box and taken to the evil Whitecoat Apecat in the whooshy car.

some Hunting in town and then get the ape-puppies from the Running Around and Shouting Place.[2]

Oh wow! This is GREAT! Can I come too, please, Great Packleader, much respect, lick lick, please, I want to come too. Please, paws up, can I? CAN I?

OH GREAT! He has my LEASH! WALKIES! Happy HAPPY HAPPY DOG! Much bouncy. Bring him a potato chip packet (any inside? No. Sad Dog).

My Packleader makes the car's tail end open wide. It sticks a bit and creaks. "Hup, Jack, in you go."

It is not so comfy as the backseat. Are you sure, Great Packleader?

"Hup, Jack, hup!"

Are you sure?

"In!"

Oh. Okay. Hup, scrabble. Turn around, clatter, knock over a metal thing, turn around, scrunch, turn around, tinkle, push a big bag of glass things out of the way, turn around. Lie down. That's better. But a bit hard and not so comfy. Also the interesting papers and bits of sandwich are in the comfy bit.

---

[2] A place to keep ape-kittens during the day so We can sleep. Apparently they learn useless things like how to make marks on white Cat bedding called paper.

I have found all the good eating stuff in the back. Okay, Packleader, you can shut the funny upswinging door.

"I've got to recycle those bottles," says Packleader.

GREAT. I like recycling. Big garbage cans with so many interesting and complex smells, mature pasta sauce, mature mayonnaise, mature ketchup . . . Yum.

"I'll do it tomorrow," says Packleader.

Sad. That means never. Or until Pack Lady notices.

Now Packleader sits in the front bit where the big round thing and the interesting sticks are. He does something with his clever paws. The car goes, *Grrrvvrrr chur chur chur.*

Packleader says bad words. He does the clever thing again. *Grrrvvrrr harooo chur chur chur.*

The car doesn't want to wake up. Why not?

Packleader barks at the car. I sit up and bark too.
RUFF RUFF, BAD CAR!

"Shuddup, Jack," growls Packleader.

Why? I was only agreeing with you.

Grrrrvvrrrr grrrvrrrachur vrrschchck-chck . . . The car does a Smoke Message out of its tail and goes, *VRRRROOOM.*

See? I was helping you wake up the car, Great Packleader.

Packleader stops barking. He plays with the interesting sticks and makes the wheel go around. The light-trees start moving past, so does the road and the NotMyPack apedog dens. Once the things are moving past, Packleader is stuck where he is until they stop. He can bark, and it's true he has a very LOUD DEEP BARK, but he can't stop me doing what I want.

Hup. I jump over onto the backseat, which is much more comfy to lie on. Also Mikey has left a pile of chips under his little seat and there is a bag with Pete's removable furs in it, a T-shirt and short leg-coverings and very splendidly strong-smelling paw-coverings, all covered in Pete-smell and mud. AAAAAHHHH. Lovely.

"Jack, go in the back. You BAD DOG."

I do not understand, Great Packleader. Why am I a Bad Dog for sitting in the comfy bit?

Packleader growls, "I've gotta get a dog grill for this car."

Hi, Great Packleader, this is FUN, look at the light-trees whizzing past. All the other cars are barking at us and going *vroom* past us. Car barking is LOUD AND IMPRESSIVE, they go BEEP BEEEP BEEEEEEEP. Packleader growls and barks back. This is FUN! I put my nose out of the window, very very windy out there, makes my nose tickle so I sneeze.

Tree tree treetretre . . . Boring. I go to sleep with a Pete paw-covering in my mouth.

Garage Dog! GRRRRR

Whooshy feeling stops. Here we are. Great Packleader does some more stuff with the interesting sticks and the car goes to sleep. I open an eye. Are we going WALKIES?

No. We are in a place with Big Food Dens and Removable-Fur Dens and Flicker-Box Dens and lots and lots of apedogs walking about and cars and two-wheels-go-fast-with-roars. Usually, Packleader doesn't like to take me Walkies in the Lots of Dens Together place, unless it's very sunny. But it isn't. It's normal cold and gray weather. Oh well. Never mind. I like saying hello to everyone too.

Packleader opens two windows so the other dogs and apedogs can hear me bark and off he goes. I sit up and watch. He's going into a big den with nothing in it except apedogs behind a glass wall who play with bits of colored paper. I have been there and smelled it. It is a strange boring place with easy-to-knock-over things full of paper. All the apedogs look sad and the colored paper game doesn't look like much fun. Packleader is always grouchy when he goes there, especially if the clicky-clacky Flicker Box stuck in the wall eats his Plastic Biscuit.[1]

Anyway, my Packleader is sensible: He gives all his colored paper to Food Den apedogs and they give him FOOD.

---

[1] This is a flat thing made of hard inedible plastic with shiny bits. Apecats become absurdly huffy when they lose them or the Big Stupid eats them up.

There are lots of apedogs going past the car. *Hi, hi there. ARROOOF. I see you, Suki, and your Pack Lady, respect, respect, much respect, how nice to see you. . . .*

Suki is a Senior NotMyPack Friend girl dog who lives near my Pack's den.

Hi there, Jack, she says, we have been to get MEAT. This is a very interesting-smelling car, may I leave a Wet Message? Respect, respect.

ARROOOF! I say. *I am sad I can't respectfully smell your very nice Wet Message, Suki. Maybe later.*

There are Bad Dogs too. OH NO, there is Garage Dog! GRRRRR ROWF ROOOF, ARRROOF GRRRRR, RUFF RUOWF. . . . I hate Garage Dog. . . .

Garage Dog yips back. He stands up on his leash and goes, *Yip yip yarp, riifff yip! I'm very Fierce, I can tear out your tum and your throat and your tail end, yip yip.*

He has an old apedog Pack Lady on his leash. She is the garage apedog's Pack Lady. She is trying to pull Garage Dog away.

GRRROOWF. GRRROWF. *I'll get you, Garage Dog. . . .*

I jump into the front bit of the car to go on barking. Put my paws and tummy on the round bit so I'm

TALLER.

BEEEEEEP!

What?

BEEEEP!

OH WOW! The car barked with me! The car hates Garage Dog too! We are a Pack!

ARFF ARFF BEEEEP ARRFFF ARRRFF ARROOOF! BEEEEEEEP!

BEEEP! BEEEP! VERY LOUD BARK. VERY GOOD.

See, Bad Garage Dog, the car is in my Pack too. It is barking at you too, ARRRRRF!

Garage Dog does a Wet Message on the car's wheel, hiding Suki's friendly one.

OH NO! HOW DISRESPECTFUL. *You*

are BAD BAD *BAD!* I jump to the back again, over the interesting sticks.

Garage Dog stands on his back legs (but he's still pretty small) and he goes, *Yip yip, yarp, I'll get you, I'll bite you and make you into meat, yip yip!*

I jump in the front again, try to get the Bad Garage Dog. My paw catches on one of the interesting sticks, ouch, hurt, pull pull, bite, pull . . .

Something goes clunk under the floor.

ARROOOF ARROOOFF ARROOOOF! I'll get my Pack Lady Petra, who is very Fierce and has her own den next to mine, and we'll come and make you into meat, BAD BAD BAD! GRROOOF BAD! . . . ARROOOOFFF!

What? What's happening?

Oh, how FUNNY! The car isn't going *vrrroomm chuchchug* like it usually does when it wakes up. It sounds still asleep. But the light-trees are moving again.

And all the big dens are moving.

OH WOW! I'm making everything go. The whole world is moving for ME!

OH WOW WOW WOW, THIS IS GREAT!

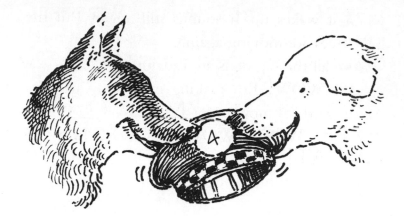

I DRIVE A CAR

Look at me, Garage Dog, pretty soon I'll bash you with my car and make you into squashed gluey meat like a hedgehog ... ARRRF ARRF! That'll teach Garage Dog to come near my car!

ARROOOF, ARF, WOW WOW WOW!

Hi there, look at me, Suki, I am Very Thick, I am driving a car! This is greeeeeeat! I am like my Packleader now! Oh wow wow wow! Bye now!

I know how to drive, it's easy.[1] You put your paws on the round thing ...

---

[1] Possibly, though not for Big Stupids.

BEEEP! BEEEEP! WHEEEEE
ARF ARRRF WOOF ARROOOOF!
GRROOOOF! ROOOOOFFFF! Very windy
again outside.

All the apedogs are barking at me, and running
away. One of them is pointing a lightning box at
me. An apedog in dark removable furs with a Bad
Headthing[2] on his head is running up the hill.

WOOOWWOWWWOWW ARRF ARRF!
This is GREAT. There is wind. We are going
FAST.

---

2 For some reason the Big Yellow Stupid hates hats.

CRUNCH! Whoops. Broke some wood with stuff on it. Oh dear. Never mind. THIS IS FUN!

Hi there, apedogs! See, I can drive too. ARROOOOFFF!

A tree in the middle of the Big Round Place is getting bigger and bigger. It has a fence around it to make Wet Messages harder. Suddenly it jumps in front of me.

Hi, tree, let's be Friends, can I leave a Wet—?

CRUNCH TWANG

CRUNCH!!

KERLANG

TINKLE

tinkle

tinkle.

OH NO! HELP!

OWCH! YOWCH! There was a HUGE BUMP! Some car fell on my nose! The car is all different! The front bit to look through is all full of big spiderwebs. So is the back. The bit with the interesting sticks is all bent. I bumped myself on something. A Wet Message happened by accident on the front seat, which is Bad Dog.

Oh dear.[1]

OH WOOW! I don't like this! Where is my car! What happened? Who did the Wet Message on the front seat?

Oh no! I am a saaaaad loooonely pupppy . . .

---

[1] You see? We were right. Cars are bad, dangerous, evil things that might suddenly move at any time, especially when Cats are sleeping on the nice, warm top part.

ARROOOOO ARROOOOO!

Help, help yelp! Packleader, help arrooooooooooOOOO! I can put my nose out of the window and smell Packleader and bark for him. ROOWF ROWF ARR-OOOOO!

I can smell him, he is upset and worried, he is galloping down the hill from the boring Colored Paper Den.

Whew. Packleader will save me from the strange bad cobweb car. He is very Big and Loud, though he runs funny from when he hurt his leg after he fell down in the Old Mill and I helped him.

Arrooo! I have a hurty, Packleader, quick, come

and lick it better! Hi there, Packleader, please SAVE ME! RRROOOF!

"Oh my GOSH!" *Pant pant. Gasp.* "What happened?" *Pant.* "What on earth happened? Are you Okay, Jack? Oh lord, look at the car. Poor Jack, is your nose sore?"

Yes, Packleader, very sore, and I think there is Jackblood too. Oh dear. ARROOOOO! Help help, Pack Lady, come and lick my nose! ARROOOO!

Packleader gets the door handle and tries to open it, rattles it hard, pulls hard, but no. It's stuck. Oh no, I'm TRAPPED. Even great big strong Packleader can't let me out, oh dear OH DEAR ARROOOOOO!

ARROOOOF ARROOOOOF

ARRRRRRRRRROOOOOO

OOOOOOOOOO!

Now a Bad-Headthing apedog with dark removable furs is talking to my Packleader. My Packleader's body says: *Tense, might be trouble, big apedog here, be respectful.*

He says, "No, officer, I'm absolutely certain I left

the handbrake on. . . . I guess the cable might have snapped. . . ."

Suki's Pack Lady comes up. Her body says: *I know all about it, I'm very clever, listen.*

"Yes, officer, I saw the whole thing. Hello, Mr. Stopes."

"Hi, Mrs. MacNally."

"You see, Mr. Stopes's lovely dog Jack . . . yes, yes, Jack, poor chap, soon get you out . . . Oh, is the door stuck? Never mind, poor poor Jack."

Hi, Suki's Pack Lady, respect, pleased to smell you again, sorry I can't smell you properly . . .

"Well, anyway, he was barking at the Jack Russell over there—just barking—and the Jack Russell was barking back—you know how they are, don't you . . ."

This particular officer apedog has a dog too. I can smell him, despite my sore nose. In fact, he smells familiar. Sniffff snortle sniffff snortle.

Yes, I have definitely smelled him before. Hmm. I wonder when? He's Big, lots and lots of fur . . .

". . . dreadful little dogs, Jack Russells, never liked them, they all think they're rottweilers and a good thing they're not, the way they go for other dogs. . . . Oh yes. Well, Jack was a bit excited and he jumped over to the front seat and back again and I think his paw must have got stuck in the brake handle because I'm quite sure I heard a *clunk* and then off he went, of course. . . . Yes, yes, poor poor Jack."

Now Packleader is doing his angry face at me. Oh dear. Why? I am a sad, sorry puppy, what did I do?

"I don't believe it. You just wrote off my ruddy car, Jack."

What is "wrote off"?

The officer's body says: *Wait till I tell my Pack*  *about this, this has cheered me up.* "Well, sir, I may need to arrest Jack for stealing a car and driving while disqualified on account of being a dog."

My Packleader makes "Ha ha ha" sounds. His body says: *Not very funny, this is a disaster, better laugh, though.* "Yeah, he's never passed a test either."

"Really. Tut tut, Jack."

Why, what did I do? What is "test"? Help, yelp! Packleader, the Jackblood may have stopped, but I don't like being in this funny car. ARRROOOO!

Packleader reaches in and pats my head. "Okay, poor Jack." He sighs a lot. His body says: *Sad, sad, sad Packleader.*

"Still, sir, I expect the insurance will cover it."

"I doubt it'll cover this."

Now the officer is being sympathetic. "That's bad luck."

"You're not kidding. And I'm due in London tomorrow."

ARROOOF ARROOOF!!! Stop barking, Packleader, get me out of here and lick my nose better!

OH WOW! SMELL! IT'S REBEL!

Packleader tries to get the other car doors open, but they are all stuck. He pulls hard, and so does the officer apedog, but the Bad squished car won't let them. Not even the upswinging back bit will open.

Oh no! I'M TRAPPED. ARROOOF ARRROO-OOO-OOO-OOOOOOO!

"Shut up, Jack!"

How can I shut up, Packleader? I am trapped in the scary funny car and my nose is sore.

I know, I will headbutt my way out. Okay, get back and bang with my head. No. Try getting back a bit more, sticks in the way, bang. No, try again.

Why is my head hurting?

The officer goes and gets something from his funny-shaped car. Oh, his dog is there, I can smell him. I know him.

RROOOFFF?

I can hear the officer's dog. He says, *ARROOOF ARROOFF, respect. I used to be in your territory when I was a puppy, I remember you!*

Oh yes. I can smell him properly now. I remember too! When he was a little puppy, he was with a Pack near where I live. He was a very nice, friendly puppy, lots of fur, pointy ears, very very big paws. I held his nose in my mouth, to show who's bigger. He did a Wet Message on the ground to show respect, I did one on the wall to show I am Senior. He did puppy-bounces and licked my face. We played running-around and chasing games. He is a Friend called Rebel!

ARRF ARRRF.

I remember. *Hi there, Junior NotMyPack Friend Rebel.*

My Packleader will help you, Senior NotMyPack Friend Jack, he says.

The officer apedog brings a metal thing and he

and my Packleader try to break the car. But the metal is all bent and it doesn't work properly.

I will help. I will summon all my Pack by howling and barking extra loud. ARRRF ARRF, ARR–OOOOF, ARROOOOOO!

Packleader is talking on his talkbone and the officer apedog is talking on his talkbone. When will you get me out of this funny car? . . . AROO–OOOO!

ARROOOOFFF ARRROFFF ARRROO–OOOO!

Garage Dog comes past with his old apedog Pack Lady. *Yip yip yarp, yer Big Nelly, can't get out, can't get out, but I can do a Wet Message saying Big Nelly on your car, yip yip.*

I hate you, Garage Dog, ARRRF ARROO–OOF, *ARRF!*

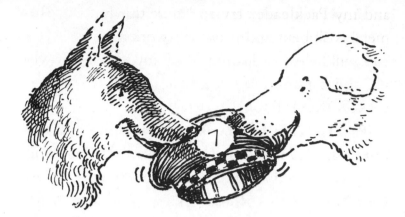

EEEEOOOOO MONSTER!

Packleader is talking to Garage Dog's Pack Lady and waving his talkbone next to his ear. I can hear Garage Dog's Packleader in the talkbone. Then my Packleader talks to the officer apedog. "Look, I've got to go get the kids from school, it's not far. . . . Would you keep an eye on Jack until the guys from the garage get here?"

"Glad to," said the officer apedog. His body says: *Good, I like dogs.* [1]

I like you too, officer apedog. I will help you get that Bad Headthing off your head as soon as I can,

---

[1] Why?

don't worry, I won't let it sit there scarily. . . . OH NO!
My Packleader is GOING AWAY. Don't leave me, Packleader,
please. I am a scared puppy, yelp yelp help!

ARRROOO
OOO
OOOOOOOOOOOOOOOOOOO
OOOOOOOOOOOOOOOOO

Junior NotMyPack Friend Rebel in the officer's
car is helping too. *Arrooof. Arroooofff!* he says, helpfully. *ARRF ARRF.* We are making a Very Loud helpful noise.

"Quiet, Rebel!" barks the officer apedog.

We bark even more.

Here come some NotMyPack garage apedogs
wearing removable furs all covered in carblood and
carjuice. They have lots of metal things that smell
of lightning and carblood.

Oh dear. Scared puppy. I can smell that this is
Garage Dog's Packleader!

OH NO. IT'S A HORRIBLE EVIL MON-
STER THAT GOES **EEEEEOOOOOO!**

Oh no, Wet Message happens again, I am a
scared puppy, help help help. Dig a hole in the seat,
hide in it, bits of spongy stuff everywhere, bite the
seat, oh dear oh dear oh dear, **EEEEOOOOO MONSTER**
COMING TO GET ME!

28

Officer apedog is on the other side where the window is a bit open. He has a biscuit.

Oh YUM, I like biscuits, thank you, thank you.

Whooops. Now he's holding my collar in his clever paw. He smells a bit scared, his body says: *Careful, Jack might bite, but got to hold him anyway. I like dogs, I will make sure he is safe.*

It's Okay, officer apedog, I won't bite you. If you say Garage Dog's **EEEEOOOO** monster has to eat me, I suppose it's Okay.

ARRRF ARRF, scared puppy, **EEEEOOOO MONSTER** IS BITING THE CAR, OH WOOOOOO!

Thank you, I like chewy sticks, they are very soothing when your tummy is frightened. . . .

More?

Ham sandwich. Yum. Spit out the apefood leaves. CRUNCH! CREAK. *SCREEELLL . . . !*

Oh woof! WOOF?

Now the door is open. Whew. I can escape.

Whew!

Pull really quick away from officer apedog, jump out of the car.

GRRR, it's Garage Dog's Packleader from the garage, talking to his Pack Lady and Bad Bad Garage Dog. . . . GRRRRR. . . . He can't catch me, lots and lots of apedogs here, run round and round, officer apedog trying to catch me.

Oh great! Chasing game! Hi there. Let's play. Puppy-bow, puppy-bow we can play catch!

Run run run . . . *Hi there, Junior NotMyPack Friend Rebel! Respect.*

My friend is sticking his nose through the window of his funny-shaped car. *Hi there, Senior NotMyPack Friend Jack. I remember you, respect! Respect! Much respect! ARRF ARROOOF!*

Roooof! I remember you, Rebel, how nice to smell your friendly smell again. Can I come in your nice comfy car and cuddle up, because I am a Scared (but Senior) Dog and I would like a cuddle.

I bark, Rebel barks. Rebel's Packleader opens the door. Rebel paws at the inside cage bit. At last his Packleader understands. Opens it. I jump in, smell Rebel's tail end—he eats Chappie and mixer, not too much, and marrowbone Bonios. He smells

31

my tail end, licks my face to say *Respect*.

Whew. Lie down next to each other where we can feel nice warm fur, whew. It's quite squashed because this is a narrow nest inside the funny car. But that's okay. More cozy. Pant pant. That's better. Rebel is giving my sore nose a nice respectful lick. Happy Happy Dog. I notice Rebel has a torn ear. Poor Rebel. I will give it a nice lick. We take turns licking hurties. Groan. So cozy. Everything is okay now.

Oh look. There's a car all bent, squashed up against a tree, how funny. I wonder why? [1]

Rebel's officer Packleader scratches his head. Then he pats Rebel's head and my head. "I wonder if you really are the softest dog on the force, Rebel," he says.

Yes, Rebel's Packleader, Rebel is very nice and soft and furry. This is much better.

---

[1] The Big Yellow Stupid's boneheadedness sometimes surprises even Us.

My Pack Comes Back

Now my own Packleader is there with the ape-puppies, who are all talking at once.

"I'd never have believed it," says Rebel's Packleader. "They're friends. Look at them."

"Aaahh, look at Jack, Mikey, he's being friends with the big police-dog puppy." Terri smiles at me and my friend Rebel.

"Oh. Is that an Action Man Brave Hero Dog?"

"Yeah, that's right. Police dogs have to arrest criminals and track down bombs and all kinds of stuff like that. . . ."

"Not all at once, Pete." Terri is doing her

I-am-nearly-grown-up voice. "They have special tracker dogs for bombs. There was a program about it after you went to bed and ..."

"Well, I bet this police dog does tracker-dog stuff when there's escaped convicts. Look how big he is, he's huge."

Mikey is holding his Packleader's hand. "He's an Action Man Brave Hero Dog, isn't he, Dad?"

"Yeah, I expect he is. But he's being nice to Jack at the moment."

"CanIyava Action Man Brave Hero Dog? With a sled? And skis and a big gun that fires rockets and lasers for the Brave Hero Dog, can I, Dad?"

"No, Mikey, not for the foreseeable future."

Terri is smiling at Rebel. "He must be a really cool dog. Usually big male dogs are fierce to Jack and growl at him and climb on his back and stuff."

The officer apedog smiles back. "Well, Rebel is a big softie, but ..."

"Rebel?" barks my Packleader. "Hang on, is that

little puppy Rebel? With the soup plate paws? Was he puppywalked by a retired couple in Trenever?"

My Packleader is strangely stupid about this. Why did he need to ask? We used to meet Rebel a lot when he was a puppy. Can't he smell who Rebel is? [1]

"That's right. Police Dog Rebel now."

"*Rebel!*" says Terri. "Wow, you've grown. He's grown, hasn't he, Dad? He's caught up with his paws."

"Wow. I can't believe it," says Pete. "Wow. Look at him. That's Rebel. Look, Mikey, that's puppy-dog Rebel. He used to lick your face clean when it was all covered in chocolate."

"No, Pete, it's Action Man Brave Hero Dog."

"Mikey won't remember, Pete, he was only a baby himself."

Rebel has smelled my Packleader, of course. He jumps out of the van, does much respect for him.

"Well, hi there, big guy, how are you doing as a police dog?"

Rebel does paws-up for my Packleader and Packleader pats his tummy. "Boy, he's big, isn't he?"

"He's certainly the biggest police dog in the

---

[1] After extensive research, the feline primatologists working on this problem have concluded that apecats are, for all intents and purposes, noseblind. This terrible condition accounts for a lot of their peculiar behavior, such as feeding Us food that is clearly Not Freshly Killed!

force," says Rebel's Packleader. His body says: *Not too pleased with Rebel at the moment, even though I love my Junior Dog.*

Terri sees Rebel's hurty ear. "Oh, poor puppy, what happened to his ear?"

The officer apedog sighs. His body says: *Embarrassed, about to look silly here, don't really want to tell Terri what happened.* "Bit of an accident."

"It's a bad tear," says my Packleader, checking out Rebel's ear. "Did he get in a fight?"

"You could put it that way."

"Wow? Really? A dogfight? What happened?"

"His ear got bitten, Pete."

"I can see that. Who by, a rottweiler? Rhodesian ridgeback? Pit bull?"

"Much worse."

"Dinosaur?"

"Er . . . no, Mikey. Human."

"Huh?"

Rebel's officer Packleader sighs. "He was supposed to help arrest some brawlers down at the Feathered Serpent by the quay. Big fight, couple of the lads that started it were off down an alley, so I warned them, then I let Rebel go."

"Uh-huh?"

"Rebel brought the ring-leader down all right, he's big enough. He was pinning him in place, like he'd been trained. And then the bad guy grabbed his neck and somehow bit his ear."

My Packleader looks at Rebel and then at Rebel's Packleader and then back at Rebel. All the ape-puppies have their mouths open, showing their teeth; only Mikey is scowling.

"The *guy* bit *his* ear?" Packleader's body says: *I don't believe it.*

"Nasty bite too . . . Oh all right. I know. I'll

never hear the last of it, either. Rebel yelped and ran away, and one of my mates and I had to grab the bloke."

"Mm-hm." Packleader's body says: *I'm desperate to laugh, but I mustn't, shouldn't make officer apedog lose face, oh dear, VERY MUCH WANT TO LAUGH.* "Well, poor Rebel, how shocking."

I don't know why my Packleader thinks it's funny. At least the ape-puppies are properly sympathetic.

Rebel's officer Packleader says, "Not much of a Brave Hero Dog, I'm afraid, Mikey."

Wow, I say to my friend Rebel. *Mikey bit me on the tummy once, but that was when he was a very little puppy and he didn't understand. I didn't know apedogs did stuff like that after they got big.*

I didn't either, says Rebel. *It was awful. Something to do with Falling Over Juice,*[2] *from the smell.*

I lick his ear for him again.

I was very frightened, says Rebel. *It is hard being a police dog, you have to be Fierce to Big NotMyPack Enemy apedogs and often they are Fierce back and bark at you and they might hit you or kick you if you don't run away. And you have to do this hard head stuff as well. But I do not like Fierce apedogs, especially when they bite.*

---

[2] Poison that apecats like to drink. It makes them act like Big Stupids—or worse!

I keep on licking his sore ear. Poor Rebel. It must be terrible, having to be Fierce so much and do Thinking too.

Mikey is still scowling. He takes his thumb out of his mouth. "No. You're wrong. Rebel is Action Man Brave Hero Dog."

We Find a Mature BONE!

Today is so exciting. So much happening. Meeting my friend Rebel! And then we got a NEW PACKMEMBER.

Another car with a NotMyPack apedog in it came to take Packleader and the ape-puppies home. Then Rebel's Packleader took me and Rebel in the back of his van. When we got home the two Packleaders did stuff with paper and snail-trail sticks, and my Packleader talked to lots of ape-dogs in the talkbone.

Rebel and I and all the ape-puppies played in the Outside, doing chasing games and jumping games and pawball. Petra was in her own Outside and we said *hi* through the fence. Her puppies have gone to be with other apedog packs now. Rebel was very respectful  because she is a Pack Lady. She smelled his Wet Message but she still preferred mine!

After Petra's Packleader called her inside, we did more running around. It was GREAT. Rebel said he  was sure there was something buried in the ground-with-NotGrass, and so we had a nice dig, and Mikey helped with his spade, and we found a Bone I lost ages ago, which was all green and nicely mature so Rebel and I lay down to enjoy it.[1]

Packleader came out to get the ape-puppies for their tea and found us and he yelped. Lots. "Oh no,

---

[1] One of the things that most clearly demonstrates the stupidity of Big Stupids is their addiction to extremely Unfresh Food. This can sometimes be useful if the Food for the Cats is a whole day old and therefore unpleasant to eat. Given the chance, the Big Yellow Stupid will eat it up and then We can convince the big Tom apecat to open another hard-shelled Food for Us. Care must be taken that the queen apecat does not notice because she is, unfortunately, not so easy to fool and will callously allow Us to starve for the night. Then We have to make the strenuous journey down the road to one of Our other apecat territories.

Charlie's flowers! She'll really kill me now! You morons, why'd you do that?"

I think it is somehow Bad Dog, digging big holes in the ground-with-NotGrass. Packleader was yelping lots and saying "Bad Bad Bad" and trying to put some of the green stuff back in the hole.

"Rebel, you're useless," said Rebel's Packleader, laughing because it wasn't his NotGrass that got dug up. "You're supposed to stop crime, not assist it."

So Rebel brought him the interesting Bone as a present to calm him down and dropped it on his foot, and then both Packleaders were barking lots. It seems nice fragrant complex-smelling green Bones don't make apedogs feel calm.[2]

OH NO, Sad Dog. Rebel had to go home. It was Very Very Sad. Terri and Pete patted him and Mikey put his arms around his neck. "No. He's *my* Action Man Brave Hero Dog."

Rebel licked Mikey's face and Mikey licked Rebel's nose, but Rebel had to go with his Packleader, of course. Mikey was doing apedog water-howling when Pack Lady got home.

Pack Lady was mad.

Oh dear. Pack Lady is VERY MAD INDEED.

Pack Lady is barking at me lots. I am a Bad Dog.

---

2 Not surprising, in view of the stench.

I am AN IDIOT. BAD BAD BAD.

Oh dear.

I have made a hole in her flowerbed and ruined all her flowers.

What is "flowerbed"?

I totaled the car.

When? What's that?

She and Packleader are going on a Big Hunt in London and SHE DOES NOT NEED THIS EXTRA NUISANCE!

What's "London"? Maybe a very very very Big Huge Food place. Can I come?

Packleader did paws-up voice for her, and got her to go into the den to relax.

Oh dear. She fell over the nice mature bone in the Sitting Room.

Oh dear oh dear. SAD DOG. What a waste! She put it in the trash!

Sigh.

Now she has to go off again. Packleader offers to go because she's tired. "You can't," she says to

Packleader. "You're not allowed to drive the company car because it's against the firm's policy. And we can't drive it to London either for the same reason, so now we'll have to get the train. I'll try and get tickets when I pick up Auntie Zoo."

What is an "Auntie Zoo"?

Welcome, New Packmembers!

Pack Lady is back again.

Hi there, Pack Lady, so glad you came back. Hi hi, wow, OH WOW, WHO'S THAT WITH YOU?

Sniff snortle snifff snortle . . .

How interesting. This is a Senior apedog related to my own Pack Lady. She is the same height as Pack Lady but her hair has stripes in it and she is a lot wider. She smells like she is a Pack Lady too, but maybe a long time ago. She has a big long bag over her shoulder and two plastic Food Hunt bags full of things.

Terri and Pete give her big hugs and kisses. "Gosh, Auntie Zoo, are you going to look after us again? Really? Wow!"

Pete looks at Terri and Terri looks at Pete and they giggle.

Mikey is hiding behind his Pack Lady with his thumb in his mouth.

"Come on," says Pack Lady. "Auntie Zoo won't eat you, Mikey."

"She's a witch," says Mikey. "Like on the telly."

"Shhh," says Terri. "That's rude. She looked after me and Pete when Mom was having you."

"Which witch is that?" asks Auntie Zoo.

"The one in *One Hundred and One Dalmatians*."

"Cruella? I don't think so. I would never ever wear fur, you know. But I am a witch, in fact, Mikey, that's very clever of you. I can make spells and charms too."

Pete's mouth is open. Terri smiles in a grown-up way. "Oh really? How fascinating."

Auntie Zoo smiles back at her. "Isn't it? Do you still like the Spice Girls?"

Terri smells embarrassed and Pete and Mikey both laugh lots.

My Pack Lady leads Auntie Zoo into the den and she comes but then she stops. "Wait a minute. We can't leave Lulu in your mom's car."

"Lulu?" Packleader is looking worried. I don't think he likes Auntie Zoo very much.

Auntie Zoo puts down her bags and lopes back to the car. She has very long legs and plastic shoes that smell very interesting and complex. She opens the back and gets a big cage out. Pack Lady coughs and looks a little embar-rassed.

"Lulu?" says Packleader again. His body says: *Oh dear.*

Oh wow! How interesting. WHAT AN INTERESTING SMELL! Snnifff snortle sniff. WOW! A FLY-ING FEATHERY?

Can I see?

"Catch Jack, Terri," shouts Pack Lady, and Terri puts her clever paw on my collar.

Back comes Auntie Zoo holding the cage up high. "Here she is."

It *is* a Flying Feathery. Very Big. HUGE. AS
BIG AS A CROW! With a huge curved beak. It
sees me and it says, **"Arrk Arrk. Bad Dog! Arrk."**

What? I'm not a Bad Dog.

A Flying Feathery SAID APEDOG WORDS!

Oh no. Scared Puppy. Run away. . . .

"Stop him," shouts Packleader, but Terri isn't
strong enough to hold me when I really want to run
away, and I DO. This is TOO SCARY FOR ME! You can't
have Flying Featheries saying APEDOG WORDS.[1]

RUN RUN

RUN RUN.

Out the front gate,

d o d g e,

run,

down

the

road . . .

RUN AWAY QUICK!

Phew. I'm tired. Pant pant. Sniff. . . . Snortle.
Snortle. Maybe there are some chips at the bus stop.

Hi there, Packleader. Are you scared of the evil

---

[1] Of course. not. They are Food.

Feathery too? It's Bad. Shall we go find a den some-where else? Oh, Okay, you can put my leash on.

Oh dear. I think Packleader is somehow mad at me. Much barking. What is "menace"? What is "dummy"? Do we have to go back to our den? Oh well. If you say so, I suppose it's Okay.

Maybe the Flying Feathery Who Talks Apedog has gone by now.

No. I can smell it in the den. Oh dear. Oh dear.

Flying Feathery!

Auntie Zoo has put the big cage on the table in the kitchen. The Scary Flying Feathery is sitting in the corner of it, biting some banana.[1] Remy is asleep on his radiator. Maisie and Muskie are not here yet. Remy opens one eye to look at the Flying Feathery, shuts it again.

"Arrk."

"Yes, I brought Lulu on the train," Auntie Zoo is saying to Pete. "In the guard's car. No reason why not, and I sat with her so she wouldn't get lonely."

"Gosh."

---

[1] This is an OUTRAGE.

"Why not a car?" asks Mikey. *"Vroom."*

"Cars are the great evil of our age, Mikey."

"Eh?" says Pete. "What, even ones with catalytic converters?"

"Even them. They still contribute to global warming."

Packleader coughs. "Speaking of which, I'm afraid Jack totaled the car and . . ."

"I know, Charlie was telling me. No problem, we'll get the bus."

Boring ape-talk. About stoves. And central heatings (what is "central heating"?[2]). And trash cans. And shops. And buses. And stuff. Boring. Sniff snortle. Wander around the kitchen.

Hi there, Flying Feathery. Er . . . can I smell your . . . ?

"Arrk. Push off."

WHUFF. Jump backward, bash into a bag, sit on it. Oh dear. Squashy grapes.

Auntie Zoo laughs, washes

---

[2] A noble and wondrous thing, inspired by Cats, which renders the cold, damp apecat lairs a little more hospitable for Us. The apecats do not keep the heat high enough, however, despite being asked politely.

them, and puts them in a bowl. Then she pats my
ears and my side. She has a nice *I-like-you* smell.

**"Arrrk arrk push off push off push off . . .
wuzzock."**

How rude.

Lots of ape–barking. "Take no notice, Jack, she's
just jealous."

Auntie Zoo strokes the Flying Feathery with
her other finger. She is very strange.

Oh, here is Muskie coming to see when he can
eat the Flying Feathery.

**"Arrk arrk ARRK ARRK NEENAW NEENAW WUZZOCK
PUSH OFF."**

And Auntie Zoo stops stroking me and strokes
Muskie. Why? I want stroking too. ME. You have
to stroke ME! Push
my head under her
hand.

"Ah . . . yeah, I
was going to ask
about the cats . . ."
says Packleader. His
body says: *She's crazy.*

"No problem. Lulu's used to cats. I have four of
them, after all. They're all friends."

"Right," says Packleader, but his body says: *Oh boy, I bet the cats eat that bird.*[3]

Muskie sits down and looks at the Flying Feathery, licks his paw.

"Arrk," says Lulu. **"Arrrk. NEENAW."**

The strange Flying Feathery sounds like a whirly-whirly-light car. *If you try to eat me, I will bite your ears off,* Lulu says with her body.

Um. Okay. I can wait, says Muskie with his body.

Oh dear. Oh dear. What can I do? Cats eat Flying Featheries. But this Pack Lady Auntie Zoo has a Flying Feathery for a Packmember. Cats can't eat Packmembers.[4] Oh dear oh dear. My head hurts.

Maisie comes in from the other room. She sits down and looks at the cage with interest.

"Arrk ARRRK. NEENAW WUZZOCK." *Bite your ears off too,* says Lulu with her body.

Hm, says Maisie with hers. *An interesting problem. The cage must open. But how?*

"Push off PUSH OFF PUSH OFF. ARRK!"

Hm, says Maisie, stepping a little closer and looking up, making chitter-chatter noises with her teeth. This means *I'm going to eat you* in cat.

Oh dear oh dear. Packmembers must not eat Packmembers. Oh dear. I will interpose myself. . . .

---

[3] Occasionally, generally by pure chance, even apecats get things right.
[4] Yes we can. We just don't always choose to.

Whoops. I bumped the table and the cage slid....[5]

Zoo grabs for it. Pack Lady grabs for it. Packleader grabs for it. They get tangled up. I try to help and Auntie Zoo falls over me. Pete yells. Mikey jumps up and down. Terri starts laughing. The cage door opens with a clang, and there are lots of feathers as Lulu flies right up and Maisie jumps at her.[6]

OH NO OH NO OH NO. BLOOD!

Gosh. Maisie got scratched on her nose by Lulu.[7] Oh dear.

Arrf arrf arrrrrrf. WOOF AROOF. You can't scratch my Packmember Maisie.[8]

Remy opens his eye and shuts it again.

Auntie Zoo has picked herself up off the floor and caught Maisie by her scruff.[9] She hisses at her. An apedog speaks cat! She says, *Hissssschhheeees-wwwwshshshs.*

---

5 Bull's-eye! The good thing about the Big Yellow Stupid is that he is pathetically easy to control.
6 A mere trial run, of course. Practicing.
7 The prey accidentally got lucky.
8 That's right, Big Yellow Stupid! Fetch! Kill!
9 Outrageously disrespectful behavior, in any apecat.

I don't speak cat so well, but it sounds very rude.[10]

Auntie Zoo taps Maisie on the nose twice.[11] Throws her down onto the floor again.[12]

Maisie is very very embarrassed.[13] Much washing.[14] Muskie is still staring because he doesn't know what to do.[15]

Maisie goes and hits Muskie on the head with her paw and Muskie runs away.

All the apedogs laugh lots.[16]

"Arrk," says Auntie Zoo, holding up her hand, and the Flying Feathery flies down and lands on her hand. She picks up the cage and puts all the food dishes and bottles and dangly things straight and then she puts Lulu back in.

Remy turns on his other side and twitches his tail.

"Are you sure about this, Zoe?" asks Packleader, who is doing tooth-showing friendly face a lot. His body says: *I wish I could stay here and watch the fun.*

"Absolutely. You go off to London and give them all what-for at the Inquiry. Especially you, Tom—the nerve of it, trying to demolish the Old Mill on the sly to get it out of the way of the

---

[10] Extremely rude.
[11] Even ruder.
[12] Who does she think she is? We must devise a method of killing her and eating her Flying Feathery.
[13] Simply appalled at the elderly apecat's lack of manners and good breeding.
[14] One must keep oneself clean, of course.
[15] Stupid boy.
[16] Traitors! There will be a reckoning.

developers. And now they want to cut down
Pencerriog Wood and put the road through there.
It's outrageous. I'll do anything I can to stop those
awful planet-wreckers!"

Oh NO! BAD Carry-boxes!

FOOD TIME. The Cats say I do not have to explain about this even though it is a very Happy Time, best time of day.

Then going Outside to do Wet Messages. The Flying Feathery Packmember Lulu is in the room where the clicky-clacky Flicker Box lives, and the sofa bed has suddenly turned into a nice nest. For me?

Oh, sorry. For new Senior extra Pack Lady Auntie Zoo.

"He can sleep with me if he's used to it," says Auntie Zoo.

Yes please. Please? I like sleeping all cuddled up and cozy in a nest. Yes?

"Do you have any idea how much that dog snores?" says Pack Lady.

Terri is helping with putting nice soft blankets in the nest for me and she nods seriously. "We don't let Jack on beds because he not only snores and makes horrible smells, he takes up all the space and you fall out."

Auntie Zoo laughs even more and pats my head. Ohhh lovely, I love you too.

Sleep time now, but in my own nest. Muskie comes and lies on my head. Maisie is busy Outside, having cat-type fun. We have inter-esting dreams where I sit on

Lulu's cage and squash it so it breaks and the Cats can get at her.

Very very early in the morning. Still dark. So early, my tummy is only a little bit HUNGRY. Packleader and Pack Lady are coming *pad pad pad* quietly down the stairs. Shhh.

OH WOW! Hi, Packleader! Hi, Pack Lady! How lovely to see you! ARRRF. ARROOF. ROOF. LISTEN TO MY HAPPY MORNING BARK. "Erro! ERRO!"

"Shuddup, Jack," growls Packleader. He looks very sad, even though he is wearing his not-yet-smelly new leg-coverings.

Pack Lady staggers into the kitchen to make Hot Brown drinks. "Oh NO! You bad cats!"

Oh dear. She has trodden on a small Flying Feathery that Maisie made into meat last night. Pack Lady does much ape-barking, but quietly, mostly about how she hates cats.

Does she? Why does she let Maisie and Muskie upstairs and not me?[1]

She picks up the feathery meat and puts it in the trash, washes her hands, sighs. She is a Sad Pack Lady.

Time for a dog to make her feel better. I lean against her legs to cheer her up, so she nearly falls

---

[1] Because she recognizes that We actually own the lair and allow her to stay while she is useful to Us (for obtaining and opening hard-shelled Foods, mostly).

over. Hi, Pack Lady, I love you.

Food? FOOD?

It's breakfast! YIPPEE! MY FAVORITE.

Pack Lady opens the hard-shelled Food thing.

SLURP SLURP SLURP, GULP, CRUNCH, YUM YUM.

Erp.

More?

Remy comes down from his radiator. Maisie and Muskie come through the cat door. They all go *Mrrup merrryow* at the Pack Lady and wind around her feet so she trips. All the cats get breakfast, though Pack Lady says they do not deserve it.

Oh Okay, I'll go Outside. Pad pad. Wet Message, Hard Message. Enemy Tomcat came yesterday. Another Cat, one of Maisie's littermates. Another Cat. Lots of Cats.[2]

---

2 Naturally, the invasion of our territory by that revolting parrot occasioned great interest among other Cats in the neighborhood. It was necessary to make it clear that We have the right to eat it first.

"Do you think they'll be Okay?" says Pack-leader to Pack Lady.

"Of course they will," says Pack Lady. "Auntie Zoo used to look after me when I was a kid."

"Jeez, what was she like?"

"Exactly the same, only much younger and skinnier. She was my mom's baby sister, and she was into the Rolling Stones, and we thought she was great. And who else are we going to get to look after three kids, a dog, and three psychopathic cats on this short notice? For nothing?"

"Okay, Okay."

Pad out into hall. What?

There are Bad square boxes with handles for carrying removable furs. This is Very Bad. This means Packleader and Pack Lady are GOING AWAY.[3]

Quick. Bark at the Bad carry-boxes, frighten them off. ARRRF. ARROOOOF. WOOF. ARROOO-OOOF.

Pring on the doorbell. It is a NotMyPack apedog, with a smoky stick. ARRRF ARRF ARRF. ROOOF. RUFF. Go away, you can't come here.

---

[3] Sometimes this is Bad for Cats because We are put in the barred box and taken to a horrible place with cages. Other times it is Good because an ape-kitten from another Pride comes to give us Food and We can do what We like in Our den.

But instead of helping me to see him off, Pack-leader and Pack Lady get the square boxes and start to follow the NotMyPack apedog.

Oh dear oh dear oh dear. Does this mean I am the Packleader while they go on a Very Big Hunt? I am not as Big as Great Packleader, but I will do my best. Maybe it's too hard. *Don't go, Packleader, I love you.*

Eeoo eeoo eeooo. Sad puppy whines. Sadness.

Packleader and Pack Lady pat my tummy. "See you soon, Jack," says Packleader.

Oh dear. What is "soon"?

Auntie Zoo is up. "Bye, Charlotte, bye, Tom," she says. "Good luck."

♥ BACON SANDWICH! ♥

Very interesting morning time. Breakfast is all different. The ape-puppies have to eat up fast and get ready because they are going ON THE BUS.

Pete and Mikey get excited. Terri hates mornings and she goes on the bus anyway. Poor Terri.

Auntie Zoo calls me and she PUTS MY LEASH ON! OH WOW OH WOW, GREAT, HAPPY HAPPY HAPPY. WALKIES. I LOVE WALKIES. OH WOW. Come on, Packmembers, hurry up, happy happy, let's go, QUICK!

WALK, walk along the hard road, sniff snortle. Suki has already had her walk. Bad Garage Dog has left a Wet Message. I do one on top and higher. *Grrrr. I hate you, Garage Dog.*

Stand at the bus stop. Chips? No. Sad Dog.

Here comes a HUGE GREAT ENORMOUS KENNEL-THAT-MOVES WITH LOTS OF WINDOWS. Arrf, arrf.

"It's Okay, Jack, it's only a bus."

Terri goes on the first bus, full of ape-puppies shouting and pushing each other and young male apedogs being threatening at each other. Scary. We get the next one. ME and Auntie Zoo and Pete and Mikey.

SO EXCITING. Oh wow! I can smell something good. I can smell . . . OH WOW! Snifff snortle sniff snortle . . . Yum. Somebody has left a bacon sandwich. MINE NOW!

Slurp.

I like buses.

Vroom chuggga
chugggaa. Whooshy feeling. Tummy turning around. Oh dear. Maybe buses aren't so good. Lie down on my tummy to stop it turning around. Gulp gulp.

"Look!" says Mikey. "I'm driving the bus. *Vrrooom. Beep beep.*"

No good. I have to unswallow. *Ugga ugga glerp.*

"Yuck, Jack," groans Pete.

Feel better now. Oh look, someone left some nice prechewed bacon sandwich right by my nose. Yum. Slurp, lick lick.

"Oh yuck, that's *so* horrible," says Pete.

Auntie Zoo is looking out the window, didn't see.

Head between paws, sigh. Don't like the whooshy feeling. Sleep now.

REBEL! Again!

Running Around and Shouting Place is here. Quick quick, let's get off the whooshy bus. Pete and Mikey say good-bye and run in being NEEEOWW things. Auntie Zoo gets my leash and off we go, boring hard road.

Walk walk. This is great. Here is a soft road, full of interesting news, lots and lots of other dog friends I don't know yet. Girl dogs. A Fierce Brown Small dog-type person eating a rabbit. Lots of Flying Featheries. Lots of Wet Messages and some Hard Messages. I leave plenty of Jack Messages so they know I've been here.

I wonder where we're going, Auntie Zoo. I know our Pack's den is that way. Why are we going this way? I can feel it's not quite the right direction. Aren't we going to get a car or a bus? You can walk from the Running Around and Shouting Place to our Pack's den, but it's a very very long way. Packleader and I did it once when the car was sick and Packleader gave up waiting for the bus back. It took all morning and we met some very fierce-looking cows.

Oh Okay. Walkies. LONG Walkies. GREAT. I can go off the leash? Oh WOW. *Sniff,* snortle, *sniff,* snortle. We  are going down a soft road at the back of some dens. Lots of interesting things here.

I know that smell! A very Big Strong (quite Fierce) dog left a Wet Message here. He was very happy and excited. I know him!

It's Rebel! Junior NotMyPack Friend Rebel!

ARROOOF? Arrf ARRF?

We are going along some fences now and the lovely friendly Rebel smell is very strong. Here he is! This is Rebel's pack territory! Sniffff.

ARROOOF?

Somebody big says, *ARRRRF ARRF ARRF!*

Yes, Rebel has smelled me through the fence, which has a little door in it, locked. I put my paws up, look.

WOW! Rebel has his own den! He has a kennel and some running-around-Outside inside his Pack's Outside. There he is! ARROOOOF! ARRF!

Rebel's Packleader is there, opening Rebel's door for him.

Hi there, Junior NotMyPack Friend Rebel. How lovely to smell you, respect for your territory, here I will leave a respectful Wet Message for you to smell.

Rebel has smelled me too. *Hi there, Senior*

NotMyPack Friend Jack, lovely to smell you too, I will smell your very friendly Wet Message later because my Packleader and I are going out Hunting now and it's VERY EXCITING!

"What's so interesting, Jack?" says Auntie Zoo. "Oh, a police dog. Are you friends?"

"Morning," says Rebel's officer Packleader.

"Good morning, officer," says Auntie Zoo.

Rebel's Packleader smiles, his body says: *I know the dog, but who are you?* "Is that Jack there?"

"Yes. Tom told me about Jack's adventures—that must be Rebel and you must be Officer Janner."

"Crashed any more cars, Jack?"

What? I do not understand Rebel's officer Packleader, much respect.

He pats my head and Rebel comes to sniff. Rebel's Packleader and Auntie Zoo do ape-barking about how she's looking after the Stopes children and so on. She laughs quite a lot about it. "Um . . . I wonder, if I keep going this way, will I come to Moonshadow Farm?"

"Eh? Oh, you mean the old Chybrynog place? Yes . . . just along the footpath, couple of miles, not very far. They've got a lot of people staying there at the moment, you know."

"Oh yes, I know. Friends of mine."

"Are they? Fancy that. Well, be seeing you. Bye there, Jack."

Bye bye, Junior NotMyPack Friend Rebel, smell you later.

Smell you, Senior NotMyPack Friend Jack. I am going Hunting with my Packleader now.

Walk walk walk. Sniff snortle, sniff snortle. This is quite a LONG WALKIES.

Soft Apedog Dens; Ape-puppies

We come out between two hedges, where there is a square wooden board on a stick with boring ape-dog smears on it. There is a large field with some Cow Messages in it.

Oh! Lots of interesting and complex smells. Many apedogs, many cars. Carblood, carjuice. Dogs. Small movable apedog dens made of cloth and some of plastic and some big ones with wheels. NotMyPack dogs come to smell me. Lots. Oh dear. They smell quite fierce and a bit like Garage Dog.

They smell my face and my tail end. Some of them growl and bark.

Er . . . hi, NotMyPack dogs, I am respectful, I am not fierce, I do not want any of your food.

Make quite small, low tail.

One of them growls. He is their Packleader.

Oh dear. Hide behind Auntie Zoo. She pats me, puts on my leash. That doesn't help, Senior extra Pack Lady. What if I have to run away from all these fierce-smelling dogs? I don't think you can run as fast as me and it's hard to drag a whole grown-up apedog.

"Karl! Karl, are you there?" shouts Auntie Zoo, hauling me back when I pull her into a big cow-pat. "Stoppit, Jack, you great dummy."

One of the Junior Pack Ladies with a big tummy sees us and comes over. She smells interesting and

complex and . . . sniff . . . snortle . . . How interesting! She is Special. Respect, Special Pack Lady.

"Hello," she says. "What a beautiful dog."

Pat pat. Hi there, apedog Pack Lady. Can I smell how Special you are? Snifff. You are very lovely-smelling.

"Jack, stop it! Is Karl in the camp yet?"

The Pack Lady smiles but she smells nervous. "Who wants him?"

Auntie Zoo smiles back. "His mother."

"Oh." She looks at Auntie Zoo. Her body says: *Gosh what a shock, his mom, wow!* "He was over at Pencerriog Wood, but they got evicted." Off she runs.

Here comes a new apedog. He is quite big and very thin, and he has long brown tails on his head, stuck together. They smell very strong and interesting. He has metal in his face: metal in his nose, metal in his ears, metal in his lip. Poor POOR apedog, how did that happen? It must be dreadfully hurty, let me lick it for you . . .

"Down, Jack."

Oh sorry. Yes, Auntie Zoo, this is your ape-puppy, I can smell that.

"Mom!" says the new apedog called Karl. "Great to see you, how are you?" Oh. How funny! His face says, *Happy*, his voice says, *Happy*, but his body says: *Oh dear, oh no, complicated, how can I get rid of her?*

Grrrr. I don't like it when apedogs say one thing in their voice and another thing in their body. It's scary. It makes my head hurt.

"Stop it, Jack. I'm very well, thank you, Karl."

Quick ape-barking. They're here because they got chased away from another place. The field with Cow Messages belongs to apedogs who like them and hate roads, so they can stay as long as they want. More come out of the soft dens and do ape-barking. All around are lots of apedogs and most of them have bits of metal in their faces. Some have metal in their tummies. It's terrible. Who did it to them?

A small girl ape-puppy comes. She is interesting to smell as well. She has a biscuit for me and she  throws it. Ulp. Yum. I like you, girl puppy, even though you have metal stuck in your poor ears too. Your Pack Lady must be very neglectful, not licking them better.

Paws up. Show tummy. She pats my tummy. She smells the same age as Pete but I haven't seen her at the Running Around and Shouting Place.

Auntie Zoo sees her. "What's your name, dear?"

"Caroline Burley."

"Is your mom called Bud?"

"Yes. Are you Zoe? She said to tell you she's coming in a minute when she's done the washing up."

"Yes, I'm Zoe. Caroline, do you think you could look after Jack for me while I say hello to everyone?"

The girl ape-puppy nods. I like her. She is small and thin but strong. Auntie Zoo gives her the leash. OH WOW, WONDERFUL, GREAT! The girl ape-puppy Caroline and I are going to play. YES!

BURGER WRAPPERS!
BAKED BEANS!

She is a very nice girl ape-puppy. She has more biscuits in her removable furs. She throws a ball to play
NotFetch, and when I drop it, she runs and gets it
for me. She holds my leash and I take her down to
the end of the field where the Message Huts are so
I can lift my leg and leave plenty of Jack Messages.

There is a kennel-that-moves, sort of half a bus,
quite short. The window is open . . . sniff, snortle . . .
definitely food. Put my head in through the window . . . ahh! Burgers—wrappings for burger,
proper ground-up-cow burger, yum, slurp. Eat

them up. I like burgers and wrappers.

We play running up and down. I find a nice Food Dish full of mature baked beans. MINE NOW. Yum yum ulp gulp erp.

Grrrr, says one of the dogs. . . . *Yer Big Soft Thicko, that's my grub, give it back.*

Oh dear oh dear. He's growling at me Very Loud. His fur is up. His tail is up. He looks very VERY MAD.

Oh no, he's showing his teeth. Quick, Caroline girl ape-puppy, quick quick, this way, there's a little path here . . . run run run.

Caroline hangs on to my leash and I pull her away from the bad NotMyPack Enemy dog, down the path, through the bushes, away from the field where the apedogs have their little movable dens. She is squeaking and laughing about how small the other dog is.

But FIERCE!

Nice mushroomy smells here. Let's have a look. Mmm. . . . Trot trot, pad pad. Badgers. Rabbits.

Oh. Suddenly we're on the hard road. Trot trot trot. Wet Message, Hard Message.

Caroline stops and looks.

Why? Oh yes, over there is a van. There are big apedogs sitting in them. They smell quite fierce and scary.

Yes, Caroline, I think you're quite right to hide under a bush. I'll hide too. Move over. They smell very fierce, don't they? Pant pant.

Oh look. Here comes Auntie Zoo's big ape-puppy, Karl. He has got his funny tails in a Bad Headthing. He smells a bit scared, a bit excited, a bit happy. His body says: *No one looking, no one can see me, yes, there they are.* He looks up and down the road, then he quickly sits in the front of the van with them. His body says: *I am being bad and liking it!*

They do ape-barking, quite quiet. It's something about Karl creating a diversion while they do over a village nearby. What is "diversion"? Maybe Food?

Caroline lies very soft, very quiet next to me. She is biting her lip and wrinkling her above-eyes skin. She smells cross.

Now Karl gets out of the van. One of the fierce apedogs leans out. He gives Karl a big, thick brown envelope. Caroline makes a little angry growl in her throat.

Karl smiles, big tooth-showing. "God, I'm sick of hippie tree huggers," he says. "Bye." He puts the

79

envelope inside his shirt, walks away.

I don't want to say hello. I think he's scary.

Caroline waits very soft, very quiet, just like a cat.[1] After Karl has gone and the van has vroomed away, she hisses in my ear, "Did you see that? Karl was getting paid off like a villain. Did you see?"

No, girl ape-puppy, I'm sorry. I don't know what you mean. Lick your poor ear where the metal is.

"Stoppit, Jack. I don't know what to do. If I tell my mom, she'll say I was imagining it. She thinks Karl's great. And Zoe's his mom. What will she say? I can't think what to do."

Poor girl ape-puppy. She smells worried. I lick her other ear.

"Oh stoppit, that tickles."

We get up and go back up the path. Caroline doesn't want to play now. Never mind, sniff snortle, wander wander. Here we are where the soft apedog dens are. There is lots of smell of Food. Is it sausages?

No. Sad Dog. Sort of things-that-look-like-sausages-but-made-of-plant.[2] Still Food, of course,

---

[1] Learn from her, Big Yellow Stupid.
[2] An abomination! Definitely not Cat food.

but not nearly as nice as real sausages.

Caroline wants to talk to Auntie Zoo, but she is busy having an argument with her puppy. "Don't be ridiculous, Karl. I went to antiwar demonstrations when I was pregnant with you. Of course I'm coming tomorrow. I wouldn't miss it for anything."

"Well, I dunno, Mom. Maybe it'll just be a small protest, pretty boring really." Karl's body says: *Bored, tense, got to make her believe me.*

Auntie Zoo smiles and ruffles his brown tails. He winces. "Oh all right. I get it," she says, and her body says: *I love you so much, my puppy.* "You don't want your square old mom spoiling your protest. Okay. I won't wave any banners, I won't march around, I won't get arrested. Is that cool?"

"Groovy, Mom," says Karl, and his body says: *Whew, close one there, my Pack Lady is stupid.* "I'll tell you all about it afterward."

Such disrespect! I growl at him, not too loud in case he hears me.

Caroline gives him a very hard stare as he goes by, but he doesn't notice because she is only a puppy. She puts her head on one side and looks at Auntie Zoo. You can see from her face she is doing the apedog thing called Thinking, when nobody is allowed to bark or howl.

Most of the apedogs are friendly and like me. They pat my tummy and say I am a bit Tubby. This is the same as Good Dog because my Pack Lady says it too. Some of them sit by the warm red Cat God[3] and make interesting and loud noises. They do the apedog Pack howling where you bang tight strings on a roundish box to make d o i o i n g sounds and howl up and down. It's good. Like in Terri's Howling and Banging Box, only not so loud and bangy. I can help, NotMyPack Friend apedogs! I can do howling up and down too! Listen!

ARROOOO ARROOO, AWOWWOW ARROOOOOO.

Caroline hugs me and giggles. I howl even more helpfully. AWWOWOoooo.

---

3 This is a mysterious creature that only apecats know how to capture so that We can delight in it. It is beautifully warm and red and makes interesting flickery shapes. It is an animal that eats wood or black rocks and it can bite Us if We pat it. One day, Cats will learn how to hunt it, and then We will dispense with our clumsy ape-servants.

The apedogs thank me by throwing sticks and bits of mud and some burned plant-stuff-Not-Sausages at me—ULP GULP—and barking enthusiastically. They even know my Pack's friendly bark: "Shuddup you stupidog." I am so Happy I made them happy.

HAPPY Dog. Sleep now.

Caroline Comes to Our Den

Oh, hi there, Auntie Zoo. And here is another Pack Lady, quite big and round with lots of interesting dangly things on her removable furs. She smells nice too. Oh, I smell she's Caroline's Pack Lady.

Hi, Caroline's Pack Lady, respect, respect, paws up, show tummy. Pat pat pat. AAAAH.

Caroline's Pack Lady, who is called Budleia, and Auntie Zoo are talking. They know each other. They once protested against nuclear weapons together. They are friends.

Oh good. I like friends. Hi, Friend Pack Lady.

It was raining, says Budleia, and their tent fell

down. Caroline's sleeping bag was soaked. She is not very well, has a bit of a chesty cough, can Auntie Zoo help?

"Yes, of course I can," says Auntie Zoo.

It is a warmy comfy feeling to see them. Lean against Auntie Zoo's legs and groan. Let Budleia pat my tummy, say I'm Tubby.

AHHHHH. Happy Dog!

It's all arranged. Caroline goes and gets a spare sleeping bag. OH GREAT! Is she coming to our den? That's GREAT! Hi, Caroline, hi, Caroline's Pack Lady, arf arf.

You know it's time to get the ape-puppies from the Running Around and Shouting Place? ARF. Arf. Don't forget the ape-puppies!

Off we go down the soft path. Caroline is squishing through the mud with her rainboots. She has her backpack. She is talking about her school in London. What is "school"? What is "London"? Never mind, here is Rebel's territory, all full of his lovely friendly smell.

Here he is with his Packleader. Oh wonderful! Happy happy happy dog to smell Junior NotMyPack Friend Rebel again!

Pull away from Auntie Zoo, run up to him. *Hi there, can I smell you? Yes, you smell very strong. I like chocolate drops. You can smell me too.*

Rebel's Packleader lets him off the leash and Rebel does puppy-bows I puppy-bow back. *Let's play.* Bounce bounce, jump jump. Run round and round. *Smell this!* Oh wow, Stripy Face. Whew chiff. A slimy. Bouncy bouncy. *Run that way.* Rabbits!

Hi there, Caroline Puppy, this is my friend Rebel. *Rebel, here is Caroline, she is a NotMyPack Friend of ours.* Sniff sniff. Run round and round.

Caroline throws a stick for him. He gets it AND BRINGS IT BACK. *Wow, Rebel, you are very clever.* It's very hard to remember the bringing-back bit when you run for a stick.

Yes, I can do that stuff, says Rebel. *It is not so hard.*

Caroline is staring at Rebel's Packleader while

he talks about Rebel to Auntie Zoo. "Um . . . ," she says in a small voice. "Um . . ." Nobody hears.

We run ahead, run round and round and round. Sniff snortle, leave Wet Message. Hi Caroline, throw a stick, please, *here you are, this is a good stick!*

Caroline stops looking worried, throws the stick, bouncy bouncy. Rebel and I are a Pack, so you watch out, Garage Dog, we'll come and make you into meat. On we go. Auntie Zoo has said good-bye to Rebel's Packleader and he calls Rebel, so Rebel goes off with him. A bit Sad Dog. It was good to play with Rebel again.

Sniff snortle. Wet Message. Grrr. Garage Dog's relative. Grrr. Wet Message on top and scrape up all the earth.

Oops. Sorry, didn't mean to hit you with some mud.

Here's the Running Around and Shouting Place. Hi, ape-puppies, hi, nice to see you, did you have a lovely day running around and shouting? Why can't I come in and . . . ?

Oh. Sorry.

Auntie Zoo shows them her friend's girl ape-puppy.

Pete and Mikey say hello to Caroline and smile at her. Pete's body says: *Oh no, a girl, I don't like them*

(why not?), but he didn't say it in actual ape-barking. WOW AWOW AWOOF! We're going on the bus again. Great! Where's my bacon sandwich? Come on, folding doors, open up quick quick. . . . Get in the bus quickly. . . . Pull Auntie Zoo to the back, where's my sandwich . . . ? Sniff snortle, check under the backseats, quick, snifff . . .

Oh. Sad Dog. No sandwich. Somebody else must have got it first. Sigh. Lie down. Much whooshiness. Ulp gulp. Glerp.

"Oh yuck," say Pete and Caroline; they say it together.

"Honk city," says Caroline, and pretends to unswallow. Pete does it too, a very good pretend. I am hopeful I might get some of his lunch, but no.

Both of them giggle lots.

NEENAW! NEENAW!

Whew, I'm glad to get off the bus now. Home again.

Maisie is sitting by the door to the clicky-clacky Flicker-Box room where Auntie Zoo is staying. She is looking up.
Inside, Lulu's cage is lying on its side with the door open. Muskie is

89

sitting on it, asleep.

Remy is still asleep on his radiator.

"Oh no," barks Auntie Zoo. "Oh no, you bad bad cats. Bad. Bad! Wicked!"[1]

She rushes into the room, Maisie runs away and Muskie wakes up and blinks. His body says: *Eh, what?*[2]

Auntie Zoo picks him up and throws him out of the room. She rushes around calling, "Lulu, Lulu."

I sniff. No blood. No feathers lying around. I don't think Maisie and Muskie actually made the Flying Feathery into meat.[3] In fact . . .

Plop. A Wet Message lands right on my nose.

"Ark, push off, bad bad bad, NEENAW NEENAW."

Auntie Zoo sees Lulu on the light and puts up her hands to catch her. "Come on, darling. Don't worry about those bad cats."

"Wuzzock, push off, wuzzock." Lulu flies around

---

[1] How, pray, is it bad for Us to entertain Ourselves by hunting a nice tasty bird clearly brought into Our den for Our benefit? What else are birds for?

[2] Nobody could call Muskie the sharpest claw on the paw.

[3] We will, of course. But on this occasion We were only having fun.

the room with Auntie Zoo putting her hands up to her. Then she flies out the door, feathers float down, her body says: *Upset, scared, bite the cats.*[4]

"Shut all the windows," shouts Auntie Zoo, rushing after Lulu, but it's too late.

"Ark ark. Wuzzock," shouts Lulu as she flies out the window.

Auntie Zoo rushes out into the back Outside, which is a bit messy, and rushes around it calling for Lulu.

Lulu sits in the apple tree with her head on one side, watching.

The Cats watch Lulu hungrily. Don't they know she is a (very peculiar) Friend?[5]

At last Auntie Zoo comes back in with her striped hair all standing on end. She smells very cross. "Pizza all right for you children?" she asks. She sounds very cross too.

"Can I have a pepperoni feast?"

---

4 Ha. Ha. Very droll.
5 No. She is Food for Cats.

"Mine's a
pineapple
and ham."
"I will
have a very
big pizza with
sausages," says Mikey.

But Auntie Zoo has found pizza in the freezer
with no meat on it. She cooks it with more cheese
and ape-plant stuff and everybody groans except
Caroline, who just looks surprised.

"Are you allowed to eat meat at home?" she says
to Pete.

"Yeah, my dad hates vegetables. He'd never eat
a pizza with all this muck on it."

"It's a green pepper, Pete," says Auntie Zoo. "Did
you read the book about the gentle dragon who
only ate vegetables?"

"Well yeah, but it's not very believable, is it?
I mean, if they existed, dragons must've evolved,
right, and they evolved with sharp carnivorous
teeth, right, and so I don't think a dragon could
ever want to eat vegetables any more than cats do,
right . . . ?"

"That's three 'rights' in one sentence," says Terri,

very Senior Packmember. "You're getting a bad habit."

"Oh yeah? Well you've got a bad habit of being snotty and spotty. . . ."

Terri kicks Pete under the table and Pete flicks green pepper at her and Mikey spits out his pizza.

ARRF ARRF ARRF, I say, interposing myself. Don't fight, fellow Packmembers. . . . Oh nice for me! A bit of part-chewed pizza, gulp.

Mikey is sad when it's going-to-bed time because he wants his Pack Lady and his Packleader.

Poor Mikey, I will give you cuddles. Here is your blankie, you lie on my tummy and suck your thumb. There. AAAAAH. I love you, Mikey. ♥♥

"Ah, bless you," says Terri.

Auntie Zoo picks up Mikey and carries him up to bed. It's Okay. He could sleep in my basket. It would be cozy and warm, we would be cuddling.

Oh well. Maybe another time.

Caroline is going to put her sleeping bag in Terri's room. Terri is being very nice to her: She is a Senior NotMyPack Friend girl ape-puppy for Caroline. Soon they are doing claw-smearing, which makes funny horrible smells, all swimmy head, and

tastes YUK! Terri
and Pete did it on
me once, made my
paws taste nasty.
Much unswallow-
ing. Pack Lady was
very cross. She said

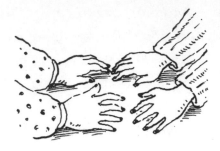

Halloween was no excuse. What is "Halloween"?
Maybe it is something to do with bags of sweets
and biscuits that you can eat if you find them first.

Later they come down in pajamas to show
Auntie Zoo. They have painted their nails all
slightly different smells. They show her, they are
very proud.

YUK. You know it isn't very nice to eat, ape-
puppies.

Also, when is it suppertime? Oh great! My
favorite. Dog food. . . .
Yum yum slurp
slurp gulp. Erp.

More?

Oh great!
MORE DOG
FOOD! WOW WOW
YES YES.

Yum yum slurp slurp gulp. Erp.

More?

"I don't believe you're still hungry, Jack, you've had two big cans."

Yes I am, Senior extra Pack Lady, Very Very Hungry. STARVING.

"Well, have a biscuit."

Gulp. Yum. Thank you, respect respect.

How Funny!

The Cats say, Leave out all the stuff about night-time and going to sleep. They were in the garden trying to catch the Flying Feathery. Sometimes there was a crashing and a lot of arking and grrooooa-owing.[1]

It was quite exciting. Right in the middle of the night Auntie Zoo went out with a net on a stick she found in the cupboard under the stairs, but Lulu was too high up. Auntie Zoo fell over one of my Hard Messages she hadn't picked up in the morning. She said lots of Packleader-type

---

[1] We were having fun.

words and shouted at Lulu. Lulu said them back. It is Scary that a Flying Feathery can do ape-barking.

Morning time was **GREAT**. I was Very Very Very Very HUNGRY. I got both front paws and a back paw cans of dog food! I LIKE AUNTIE ZOO. SHE IS A GREAT PACK LADY.

Then, after Terri gets her bus, we go on a great bus ride. Caroline comes too—bacon sandwich? Oh. Somebody else ate it. Sad Dog.

Running Around and Shouting Place? Oh, how funny. No ape-puppies? No apedogs? Empty Outside?

Gosh. Wow. We could run around and bark in it!

Pete stares at the place and then he bangs his head with his clever paw. He digs in his bag for putting chocolate and chips and stuff in. He gets some paper from the bottom of it, quite a lot, some with squashed Mars bar on it. Yum, drool. Mine? For me?

Pete smells each paper, wrinkles up his eyes when he finds one. "Oh no, I forgot."

"Forgot what?" Auntie Zoo is tapping her foot and looking very annoyed.

"Um . . . it's an in-service day. Staff training or something. There's no school today. Here's the note."

Auntie Zoo holds the paper by the corner and looks at it as if it has a bad smell, which it doesn't, it's just treeish like all paper. With a bit of mature Mars bar. And some chips. Quite nice in fact. "This is from two weeks ago."

"Um . . . yeah. I forgot. Sorry."

"No school?" asks Mikey. "Why not? I like it."

"Just today," says Pete. "The teachers are learning stuff about being teachers."

Mikey nods. "I could help them."

Auntie Zoo does a big puffing out-of-breath that apedogs do when their puppies have been stupid. "Why didn't you tell your mom?"

"Well . . . I forgot. I meant to give it to Mom, but we played football against Bosdrear and we won two to one and I was telling her and I forgot. I was going to."

"Can we go to Disneyland now?" says Mikey.

"No, we're not doing that. We're going to a sort of . . . well, sort of a party. That's what I'd planned to do today, so that's what we'll do. You'll just have to tag along like Caroline. Make sure you behave yourselves."

"Oh, Okay. What sort of party?"

"A protest against the road builders."

"Wow! Cool! Will there be security guys? And tree people? And riot police?"

"No, there won't, or I wouldn't dream of taking you! This is a *peaceful* protest. Come along. This way."

Off we go down the hard road and then the soft road, and Caroline is telling Pete and Mikey about protests and how she's been on loads with her mom and how you just march up and down shouting stuff and maybe hold a banner and get your picture taken for the paper with a policeman and stuff. Pete smells sad that he hasn't done that.

Oh yes! I can smell where we are. I can smell my pawprints and Wet Messages from yesterday, and Rebel's too. This is GREAT!

Auntie Zoo pats me. I go check if Rebel is here. No, Sad Dog, he's out. I leave a respectful Wet Message for him, find a lovely Hard Message he left under a bush.[2] Very Strong Dog. Likes Chappie. Chocolate drops.

The ape-puppies are very excited about going to a demonstration and run up and down and round and round. ARRF ARRF. Chase. Throw sticks. No, Pete, I don't know what you mean. What is "fetch"? Then Mikey gets tired and has to have a rest. Auntie Zoo gives him a piggyback ride.

When we get to the field with the soft apedog dens, quite a lot of the apedogs are not there. Nice smells of cooking and fires. Caroline's Pack Lady, Budleia, comes to say hello, pats me all over. The Junior Pack Lady who is Special, called Poppy, brings some of that big soft paper with ink smudges that apedogs like to smell at breakfast time.

"Is he the dog in the paper?" asks Poppy. "Look. Driving a car."

"Yeah, Jack did that and busted the car," said

---

[2] Aren't Big Yellow Stupids disgusting?

Mikey proudly. "It was all smashed. *Vrooom, crunk peeeyong!* Like that."

Auntie Zoo and Pete and Caroline look.

"Hey," says Pete. "It *is* Jack. Look. That's definitely him all right, he's barking."

" 'Shoppers were running for their lives when Jack the Labrador went for a spin in his master's car . . . ,' " says Auntie Zoo in a funny voice.

"And there's the car. Crunched. You look cool in your photo, Jack, you look like you were steering with your paws on the wheel," says Pete.

What is Pete talking about? What is "steering"?

He holds the paper under my nose for me to smell—it's got big smudges on it, but is not edible. In fact it smells quite poisonous. Why is it interesting, Junior Packmember? Maybe there is food inside it, like chips? Chomp, snortle . . .

"Hey, don't eat it!" Pete pulls it away. "Bad Dog."
Why? I only made a little hole.

Auntie Zoo is asking about her ape-puppy and the other apedog friends.

"It's a nuisance we got evicted from Pencerriog Wood before we were dug in, but there it is. Karl's gone ahead to organize everything, get some people up the trees, make sure the press know what's going on," says Budleia. "The rest of us'll go in the van when it comes back."

Auntie Zoo hangs my leash on a little branch and goes with Budleia. Caroline takes Pete and Mikey off to see the tents and how to make a bender. What is a "bender"? Food maybe? Pull, pull, break the branch, go for a nice sniff around.

YES! IT'S FOOD! Sniff snortle. Yum. Mature macaroni with ketchup. MINE NOW. Slurp, ulp, gulp.

GRRRRRR . . .

Oh dear. Oh no, it's the Bad NotMyPack dogs. They're hackles-up, tail-waving high, growling, tooth-showing. *We will tear out your throat for eating our Food, we are a Pack*, is what they're saying.

Oh dear oh dear oh dear. Run away. Hide behind Auntie Zoo, who is talking to Budleia.

"You dummy, Jack. It's only a . . . miniature dachshund crossed with whippet, maybe?"

"Who knows? Gandhi, stop it. That's enough, you bad dog."

Turn you into meat and eat you! WOOOF WOOF, says Gandhi.

He is a Very Bad Dog, but I make little puppy, hide because he is FIERCE like GARAGE DOG. Oh dear. Bud is big, I'll hide behind her.

"Poor Jack, he doesn't seem very popular."

"They're jealous of him getting his picture in the paper," laughs Bud. "Really, Jack, you're four times his size."

Yes, but he's VERY FIERCE.

"No, he's probably eaten their food. You wouldn't

believe how much that dog packs away," says
Auntie Zoo.

"Well, yes I would. He's a Labrador, isn't he?"
asks Bud.

"I don't understand how he can be hungry. He's
already finished all the food Charlotte left for him."

"Mm. You're a softy,
Zoe. Don't you know you
can't feed Labradors on
demand? They get circular.
He's already a bit tubby."

Pant pant. Everybody says
I am Tubby. This is Good. I
am a Good Thick Tubby Dog.

"I was going to leave him here to play with the
other dogs, but that may not be such a good idea,"
Auntie Zoo says.

"No, I wouldn't do that with Gandhi around.
Jack can come with us and help protect Pencerriog
Wood. After all, it's near where the Stopeses live. I
expect he's visited every tree in it at some time. It'll
be a good angle for the *South Cornwall News*—they
always like a nice animal picture if they can get
one. We could put a sign on his back: I CAN'T GO
WALKIES ON A HIGHWAY!"

Walkies? Yes, Walkies! I love Walkies. WHERE? NOW? Oh please, I love Walkies.

Auntie Zoo laughs. "Come on then, Jack, let's get in the van."

Oh wow. A sort of tiny bus. Maybe bacon sandwich? Burger wrappers?

GREAT! Chips! Snortle, chomp, lick, sneeze. I like buses.

Everybody gets in, budges up. Pete and Caroline are sitting next to each other, talking about demonstrations, Mikey is sitting on Auntie Zoo's lap, sucking his thumb. She is telling Bud about the Cats nearly catching Lulu and Lulu escaping.[3]

Caroline is still telling Pete about demonstrations. "My mom took me to a sit-in in the city too. There was a party there. It was wicked."

Lie down under Pete's legs. Slurp lick. Very thirsty now. I wonder why. Oh dear, whooshy feeling. I don't like buses when they go whooshy. *Vroom.* Light-trees and ordinary trees going by. Much bumpiness at first, then it's smooth, then it's bumpy again.

"Hey," says Pete. "I know this road, we're nearly

---

[3] Not so. No mere bird Dinner could really escape Us. We merely let her go so We could have more fun later.

home. This is near our village. Look, there's a sign for Trenever. Great. You can stay the night again, Caroline—can't she, Auntie Zoo?"

Auntie Zoo and Bud look at each other and smell of going-to-laugh, but they don't. "Of course," says Bud.

"Are you stopping them knocking down the Old Mill again?" asks Pete.

"No, that's legally protected now. Thanks to your mom and dad."

"I know. That's why they're up in London. So Dad can be a witness at the inquiry and Mom can do lawyer stuff and give 'em all what-for. That's what Dad said."

"Well, now they're trying another route for the road. The trouble is they're going to fell this beautiful old woodland called Pencerriog to make room for it. . . ."

"Oh, I know Pencerriog. It's not that beautiful. It's only a load of old trees," says Pete. Everybody stares and he goes red and uncomfy, as if he ate something that belonged to the Packleader. "Well, there's lots of trees around, aren't there?"

"Some of them are quite rare and there's the wildlife—rare amphibians and a couple of rare species of butterfly," says Bud in that I'm-quite-

106

cross-but-trying-to-sound-friendly voice that Senior NotMyPack Ladies often have.

"Oh. Right," says Pete, nodding a lot. His body says: *Oops, embarrassed in front of a girl ape-puppy.*

The other apedogs start talking again, about the time when they went to support the tunnel diggers and the time when they all hugged trees. . . .

"You've got to remember," whispers Caroline to Pete. "Trees are good, roads are bad."

"Why?"

She stares at him. "They just are. It's not something you argue about."

"Why not?"

"You just don't. It's ecology."

"Oh. Mom says there isn't anything you can't argue about, except not with her in the morning or no TV."

"Well, you can't argue about trees. It's like not eating meat."

"What?"

"Eating meat is wrong. You can't eat meat because it's wrong."

"Why?"

"It just is. You wouldn't want to eat a little fluffy lamb."

" 'Course I would." Caroline gasps. Pete frowns. "I like lamb, specially with garlic and rosemary. Dad does this really great roast[4] with potatoes and stuff and . . ."

"Ugh."

"It's not ugh, it's nice. Anyway, you don't eat them when they're little and fluffy, you eat them when they're a bit bigger, right? And they wouldn't be there at all if we didn't eat them. You can't keep sheep as pets, they're too stupid."

"It's just wrong because animals are people too. . . ."

"No they're not. Have you ever tried talking to

---

[4] Roasting is an appalling apecat custom: they put delicious food for Cats in a very hot cupboard and burn it until it is unrecognizable, and then they put plants with it and eat it all up and give the Cats hardly any, no matter how politely We ask, so We have to wait until there are no apecats about and the Big Yellow Stupid is near enough to take the blame.

a sheep? Even Jack's brighter than a sheep. They're not people."

"Well, they're like people."

"But they're not."

"And it's disgusting to eat carrion, dead things."

"Why? You eat dead plants. Have you ever actually tried any meat?"

"I'm not allowed. . . . Except the hot dog I had once at a demonstration, which wasn't really proper meat. My mom says I mustn't. I have to eat loads and loads of lentils and tofu and stuff instead."

"Ugh . . . lentils! I hate them."

"So do I."

"But that sounds awful. So you've never eaten a ham sandwich or a burger?"

"I had a hot dog. That's like it."

"It's nothing like it. Never?"

"Never." Caroline shakes her head.

Pete holds her paw with his clever paw. "Well, I say that's terrible. Tell you what. I'll get you some proper food so you can try it yourself. Then you'll know if you like it or not."

Caroline frowns at him but she doesn't smell annoyed, she smells pleased. Her face looks like it's doing that ape-thing called thinking. "When my mom's not looking."

"'Course. I'm not stupid."

"Okay then. I'll try it."

"Great. Do you like soccer?"

They stop talking about food, which is interesting, and talk about football, which is boring. I like playing football, though: the ape-puppies kick a big ball to each other and you bark at it and chase it and paw it and bite it and turn it into a rag and play rag with it.

FUN!

Sleep now.

Oh Dear. Scary Fierce
Male Apedogs

Here we are, off we get. Sniff snortle, sniff sniff. Oh!
I KNOW THIS PLACE. It's full of lovely Jack-smells. This
is the Special Good Walkies Place when Packleader
is tired of marching around the house drinking Hot
Brown Stuff. It's a HAPPY HAPPY place. Lots
of nice trees for Wet Messages and bushes to hide
Hard Messages, and humps and bumps in the earth
to run up and down and mushroomy smells and a
stream with mud for making your tummy feel tickly
and interesting NotFurries in the water and lots of
good Messages from all my NotMyPack Friends.

WOW! WHAT BRILLIANT WALKIES!

It's GREAT here, only not the badgers because they're Fierce and might bite.

Sniff snortle. I can smell dug-up earth. The apedogs have been digging a lot. Maybe they could smell bones! Can I have some? I like mature bones!

All the apedogs are milling around, ape-barking. Some of them are young male apedogs, smelling

very aggressive and fierce. They are in a pack. Then there are older male apedogs and female apedogs. Not many ape-puppies. Some of them have flappy things on sticks with paint on and old nest-coverings with paint.

ROOF ROOOF ARROOOF. There are apedogs climbing in some of the trees, just like Cats.[1] It's so clever. I tried it once and I got stuck

---

[1] Mostly done by ape-kittens. It shows they really are basically monkeys, as anyone with half a nose can easily smell. However, they are not nearly as good at it or as graceful as Cats. Big Stupids are unable to climb even the simplest of trees and fall entertainingly into brambles if they try, pulling the Tom apecat down with them.

and Packleader had to come and get me down on a ladder. He says I nearly crippled him.

Over in another field are some cars and big trucks. There are more apedogs there, another pack. They have got Big SCARY RRRRRR things for cutting trees. Then there are apedogs in between. They are wearing dark removable furs and Bad Headthings like Rebel's Packleader. Some more apedogs come with boxes on their shoulders and start talking to the boxes. NotAnybody'sPack.

This is all very interesting. Is there Food any-where? Sniff snortle.

Auntie Zoo sees the young male apedogs and frowns. "What are they doing here?"

Bud looks, frowns, and her body goes: *hate you!* "Oh, not again." She starts to smell scared-fierce, like all Pack Ladies do when their ape-puppies might be in danger. "Karl promised me he wouldn't tell them about this. . . ."

"*Karl* invited them?" says Auntie Zoo. She puts my leash on a tree branch and marches over to where Karl is talking to some young apedogs with no hair who have come in another van.

Sniff, snortle. Squirrel in this tree. Yum (but very Fierce, with Big Teeth). Wet Message. Oh, George and Fido III have been here recently. Hard Message for them as well.

Auntie Zoo is talking to her grown-up puppy. I can't hear what they say very well, but their bodies say:

Auntie Zoo: *Angry, you bad puppy!*
Karl: *Angry, not your puppy anymore, what are you doing here? Disrespect.*
Auntie Zoo: *You bad bad puppy, this is bad, those male apedogs are bad.*

Karl: *My Pack, they're Okay. We are going to do fighting. I like fighting. Not your puppy anymore.*

Auntie Zoo: *Bad puppy, what about the apepuppies over there and Jack?*

Karl: *Not your puppy. Oh no, why are they here? Oh no.*

Now I can hear them because they're both shouting.

"I told you not to flipping bring them, Mom. I told you, why can't you just once believe . . . ?"

115

"Why should I believe you when you lie to me? You told me you wouldn't get mixed up with that group again. This isn't a peaceful protest against a road anymore. Your friends are here for a fight. You silly boy, do you think you're going to keep the press on our side . . . ?"

"Oh come on, Mom, can't you? Remember your antiwar demonstrations? You've bored me about them often enough. Violence is a necessary tool of political protest. . . ."

"No it isn't. It doesn't work. And what about the kids?"

"Do what you like with them. I told you not to come. It's your fault for bringing them."

Auntie Zoo goes and talks to Budleia, and she gets mad too. *She* goes and talks to Karl and Karl is very disrespectful to her. All the Senior Pack Ladies talk to each other, but not the Junior Pack Ladies, who are admiring the male apedogs and talking to them.

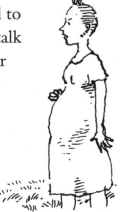

Then Budleia goes and barks at Poppy, the Junior Pack Lady who is Special, and Poppy looks angry. Her body says: *No, I won't, not your puppy. I'll stay here with all these nice young male apedogs.*

Caroline and Pete and Mikey have found some red unripe blackberries and are talking about whether you can eat them yet. No you can't, ape-puppies. Can't you smell that? Push them away from the Bad Food with my nose.

Pete has seen the young male apedogs with no hair. "Wow, look. Don't they look cool?"

"Oh, them," says Caroline. "They think they're so big and strong. My mom says they're just stupid hoodlums. They don't really care about the environment or anything except a good punch-up."

What is "punch-up"? Food?

"Great. I've always wanted to see a real punch-up." Pete's body says: *Uh-oh, might be scary.*

 Auntie Zoo comes over to them. "Now then, children, I'm sorry, but I've made a mistake bringing you here. I didn't realize there was going to be trouble."

"Right," says Pete, looking very excited. "Like a big riot?"

117

"No, not a big riot. But it might get nasty."

"Wow. Cool!"

"Can I get my light saber?"

"No, Mikey, you're not going to be here. Caroline and Pete are going to take you and Jack straight home."

"Owww."

"What, now? Just when something might happen?" Pete is disappointed.

"Don't argue."

"Can I come back when I've taken Mikey home?"

"Certainly not. You have to stay with Mikey and look after him, you and Caroline. Understand?"

"But I've never been in a real riot. . . ."

"And that's how it's going to stay."

"Are we going by ourselves, without you?" says Caroline, and her body says: *Thinking lots.*

"It's Okay," says Pete, very Packleaderish. "It's only about ten minutes' walk and there aren't any four-lane highways or busy roads, not like London. I came here every day to get horse chestnuts last autumn."

"Oh." Caroline looks impressed.

Auntie Zoo says, "Now, you've got to be responsible, Pete. I'd come with you if I had a car, but

I daren't leave yet in case Bud and I can head off the trouble. Bud certainly won't go until she's got that silly girl Poppy away from here. So here's the front door key. Off you go. Straight home, no detours."

"What about you?" asks Pete.

"I'll be along as soon as I can."

Special Poppy is with Karl, giving him a cuddle. Oh wow! Karl is her Packleader! Wow! How interesting. Like with me and Petra.

"Can you manage that, Pete?"

"But I . . ."

"Or I'll just have to come with you and then Poppy might get caught up in whatever happens and she might get hurt and so might her baby."

Pete makes *tsk-tsk* noises. He looks very sad. His voice is sad. But his body says: *Whew, maybe a real fight with those big male apedogs in it might be too scary.*

"Oh Okay," he says, lots of whining in his voice, but now his body says: *Hey, we can do naughty stuff now, great!* "Can I have some money to . . . to get comics at the shop?"

The apedogs with RRRR things are starting to move this way. Auntie Zoo looks worried. She really wants to get rid of the ape-puppies. "Yes, all

119

right. Here's a five. And I want the change. I'll join you at the house just as soon as I've talked some sense into these silly kids."

"Okay." Pete gets my leash. "Come on, Jack, let's go."

Oh NO! Stranger!

Okay, Pete, as I am Senior Packmember, sort of Packleader, I will go first. (Get away quicker from all those fierce-smelling apedogs. I didn't know apedogs did fighting like that. It's scary. They're Very Big.)

Pete holds my leash. Caroline holds Mikey's hand. We go down a little path that Pete knows and I know from coming here with Packleader. I can smell my old trail from last week, it's easy. Off we go. To the shop. GREAT!

There is some loud barking from the apedogs,

all together. It's scary. Let's run, ape-puppies, quick, this way.

Look here, ape-puppies, what a lovely deep-smelling mud wallow. Big Furries with clip-clop paws have left Hard Messages here. Isn't it delicious? Come on. Let's lie in it and wear the nice fragrance, so the Bad apedogs can't smell us.

"No! No, Jack, don't go in the . . ."

SLURP, AAAHHH . . . Lovely cool tickly mud on my tummy. Ahhh.

". . . mud. Oh no."

"Jack did it again, Pete," says Mikey. "Look, he likes it. Shall we try it?"

"No way, Mikey. You wouldn't like the smell."

"Chocolate-coated labrador." Caroline laughs again. "Phew. He stinks."

"We'll have to hose him down when we get home."

We come out of the path and onto the hard boring road. There is the shop. I like it. It's a Big Food Place where they have MEAT. But I can't go in. I don't know why. I would be very good at getting all the Food. YUM.

Pete puts my leash on the railing. He and Caroline and Mikey go in. They are a very LOOONG time. Yawn. Boring. There is a strange van over there. With NotMyPack apedogs in it, talking and eating smoky-sticks. They smell nervous.

Ruff ruff.

Oh, here is a Senior NotMyPack Friend girl dog. *Hello, Suki, did you have a nice walk?*

Yes, thank you, Jack, I smell you found somewhere interesting to lie down.

Yes, it's that way, isn't it complex and delightful?

Mmm, yes. Horse Message and some Rabbit Message too, I think. With overtones of blackberries.

And dead leaves, of course, Suki, you can't beat dead leaves for that earthy undernote.

Very true. Here is a respectful Wet Message for you, Jack, I have to go with my Pack Lady now, respect.

Sniff snortle, lovely, she has given you Steak, I smell, how lucky you are to have such a generous Pack Lady, respect.

Bye, Jack, smell you later.

Here come the ape-puppies. They are talk- ing and smell- ing very excited. They have a bag of FOOD. FOR ME? Thank you, thank you, ape-puppies, clever, strong ape- pupies, all by your-  selves you have hunted me lots of splendid MEAT!

"We were lucky there was so much in the cut-price basket. Now you can try all of them," says Pete. "No, not for you Jack, down."

Why not?

Off we go now. Pete lets me off the leash because he doesn't like the nice mud wallow fragrance.

I run ahead to our Pack's den. . . .

STOP!
BADNESS!

What is this?

Sniff snortle, sniff SNIFFF.

GRRRRR. A Stranger Smell! There is a NotMyPack apedog in Our Den! He is picking up stuff and carrying it to the door, which is open.

GRRRRR. You can't have Our Den, NotMyPack enemy apedog. GRRRRR,

I am a Big (quite Fierce) Smelly Dog, I will BITE YOU . . . GRRRRRR. Stand between my ape-puppies and the den. Hackles up. Make myself EVEN BIGGER. Little slitty eyes. GRRRRRR.

Pete and Mikey and Caroline stop because I am in the way. They try and push past. I stand on my back legs and push them back. No, no, apepuppies, you can't go there, BADNESS! It's a NotMyPack Enemy apedog in

OUR DEN!

They start getting cross with me. Then they see that the Flicker Box is outside on the ground and the front door is open. They stare openmouthed while I growl. Caroline says, "Quick, hide."

Pete gets my collar and drags me backward and we duck down behind the hedge. The NotMyPack Enemy apedog comes out with Terri's Howling and Banging Box and puts it down. Pete puts his hand around my nose so I can't bark at him. Why? Next door there is another Enemy apedog, putting things on the front step.

OH WOW!
WHAT'S HAPPENING?

"Wow," says Pete. "Burglars!"

"I know him! And him! They were giving money to Karl yesterday. Like I told you last night," says Caroline.

"They must be doing the whole village at once while the police are busy with the protest."

"Won't more cops come?"

"Not in time. Not all the way from Liskeard, they can't. My mom was telling my dad she'd heard about this gang that specialize in tying up all the local police with an accident or a pub brawl or something, so they can't come when the burglar alarms go off, and then they rob every house in the nearest village as quick as they can; they make a fortune."

"Ohh. What if somebody's there?"

"They knock 'em down and do it anyway. They're a nasty lot, my mom says."

Pete and Caroline look at each other and then grab Mikey, who is going toward Our Den scowling and waving his fists and shouting, "You can't have my telly!"

"No, Mikey. Come on, run."

Very good thinking, Pete, run away from the Bad Enemy apedogs.

Pete and Caroline and Mikey run back to the

shop. They forget to put my leash on the rail. I can hear them saying stuff, their voices all sharp and excited. Makes my hackles go up. The man in the shop has a talkbone, he is talking to it. I guard the door. Grrrrrrrr. You can't come in, this is my territory, I am guarding my ape-puppies.

The van with the Enemy apedogs in it goes down our road and stops. Another Enemy apedog puts our Flicker Box in the back. What are they doing? Caroline comes outside, stares hard at the back of the van, and goes in again, muttering.

Why are we waiting, ape-puppies? I don't think we've run far enough, apedogs can run quite fast (though not as fast as me) and we could be miles away by now, which would be good, I think. ARRRF ARRF. Shall we run away a bit more?

Hunting with Rebel!

ROOOF ROOOF ARROOF
GRRRRROWF.

Here comes another van, very fast around the corner. I smell . . .

OH WOW!
OH GREAT!

It's Rebel! And his

Packleader! JUNIOR NOTMY-PACK FRIEND REBEL!

Hi there! ARRRROOOF ARRRF GRRROOOF! *Shall we play, Rebel? ARRRF?*

Rebel smells very excited and strong. He is doing serious stuff. He is Hunting with his Packleader. He does one serious WOOF so I know what's happening.

Rebel's van goes down our road. Then the Enemy apedogs' van vrooms out of it very fast, goes around s c r e e e e l the corner and vroooooms away. The back is still open and a Flicker Box falls out onto the road and smashes.

Where are all the little dogs and apedogs in the Flicker Box? It is just metal string and glass and stuff. How funny. Where did they go?[1]

Here comes Lulu, Auntie Zoo's Flying Feathery. She is flying around going, *"NEENAW NEENAW."*

---

[1] Obviously you weren't quick enough to catch them, Big Yellow Stupid. What a pity We weren't there. Feline primatologists have long wondered if the very small apecats inside the Flicker Box would be fun to play with and tasty to eat.

ARRF! Don't mess up Friend Rebel's Hunting!

I can hear Rebel's Packleader. He says very loudly, "This is the police with a dog. You have one minute to come out or the dog will be sent in to find you."

Two enemy apedogs come over the fence at the back of Our Den and see Rebel! He looks FIERCE. They start running down the road to the path. Rebel is after them! Rebel is Hunting! Arroof. ARRRF? *Can I help your Hunting, Rebel? Did you know there are many Bad apedogs?*

ROOF, says Rebel as he runs past on a very long leash with his Packleader running behind. It means, *Okay, you can hunt with my Pack.* I run after Rebel.

Lulu says, "NEENAW NEENAW," and flies round and round in circles.

I can hear my ape-puppies shouting at me, but I'm too excited to listen because I AM HELP-ING MY FRIEND REBEL CATCH THE BAD APEDOGS WHO WENT IN OUR DEN! ARRRF! ARRRF!

Run run run run after the Bad apedogs, so excit-ing, so happy, hunting with my Friend Rebel. . . .

Round the corner. Where are the Bad Enemy ape-dogs? Sniff snortle sniff snortle. Rebel is smelling for them too.

"Jack? It was *your* house. Go home, boy."

Sorry, Rebel's Packleader, but you are not *my* Packleader and I am helping Rebel. Sniff snortle. Whoops. No, you can't get my collar. I know about clever paws. Dodge, run. Sniff snortle.

Ah yes, frightened fierce mature male apedog smell in the air, foot smell on squashed grass with

many other feet. . . . Rebel can smell them too. He growls. Goes down the path. I go with him. Pad pad now, following the exciting smell. Here it is, smells very strong. They stopped running here. Splashed through the delicious mud wallow, went on. They smell not-so-scared. They think they've hidden their scent.

Very very strong male apedog smells in the air: double. Hmm. Interesting. I wonder why. . . . Ah. Maybe they came this way before. I think they did.

There is old Bad apedog smell here too. They came from over there. . . .

A Big Furry with clip-clop paws came. Female. Sniff snortle, snifff snortle. *Smell the Big Furry. Rebel, can you smell her?*

Yes, I can, says Rebel, *but we mustn't get distracted. We must follow the Bad apedogs. This way.*

My Friend Rebel is Very Clever. It is hard to keep on thinking about one thing.

His Packleader is saying nice encouraging things to him. But "Go home, Jack," he says to me.

But he is not my Packleader, so I don't have to do it. And he is busy helping Rebel hunt the Bad apedogs so he hasn't got time to catch me.

I can hear that Pete and Caroline and Mikey are also following, quite a ways back because they don't want anybody to know they're there. They hide behind bushes and whisper. They are being a Pack too.

OH! THEY ARE OPENING A MEAT-SKIN. YUM. Ham, I like ham. Pig with smoke on it. Go back, follow the lovely smell, round the corner, into the bushes.

Hello, ape-puppies, can I have some MEAT? PLEASE?

"Go away, Jack," whispers Pete.

Sorry, Pete, I do not understand. Maybe it would help if you gave me some MEAT.

Caroline is munching it with a thoughtful expression. "Very salty," she says.

"Shhh," says Pete. He gives me some ham.

Mikey pats me. "You go help the Action Man Brave Hero Dog," he says. "Go on."

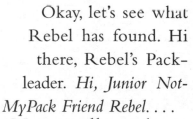

More Food? Oh, thank you, Mikey.

Okay, let's see what Rebel has found. Hi there, Rebel's Pack-leader. *Hi, Junior Not-MyPack Friend Rebel.* . . .

You smell good, says Rebel. He licks my chops and I burp for him. His

Packleader reminds him about Hunting.

Oh, the trail stops. Where did they go? Sniff snortle this way. Sniff snortle that way.

Smell, says Rebel, very happy. *They went that way, then they came back and went this way. Down this little path here. They doubled back.*

How clever of you, Rebel, respect for Junior Dog. That was puzzling for me.

This is a very little path. Rebel goes ahead much faster because the smell is so strong. His Packleader is running behind him, I am running.

Whew, it's a bit pant-making, running like this. Rebel's Packleader is very strong. He is not as big as my Packleader but my Packleader would be going *hur hur hur* by now and coughing.

The path comes to the wood. Oh dear. One Bad apedog went that way. One Bad apedog went the other way. Many ways. My head feels tight with all the hard thinky stuff.

Rebel stops, points with his nose. *Would you follow that apedog and bite him if you catch him, Senior NotMyPack Friend Jack?* he says, very respectfully.

Oh dear. I've never bitten an apedog. What if he is Fierce? What if he bites my ear?

Oh dear.

But I can't let Rebel think I'm not as brave as

he is, especially when I'm not.

Okay. Sniff snortle sniff snortle. Follow the other trail, even though my tummy is going whirly whirly.

The Bad apedog is going right through the wood toward where all the apedogs in the trees and the other apedogs with RRRRR things are barking at each other. Oh, I smell. He is one of the apedogs that Karl talked to yesterday in the van. He is a Friend of Karl's. He is going this way, very clear strong smell in the air, fierce male apedog. . . . Now not so scared, he thinks he will be safe.

Ha, Bad apedog. Not with Me on your trail, I will (probably) bite you and anyway I can
BARK VERY VERY LOUD.
ARRF.
What's that?

<small>WOOOF</small> WOOOF WOOOOOOF.

I can hear Rebel's deep bark. He is angry and scared. There is ape-barking and thumping.

Oh dear. Very confusing. Which do I do? Go

after the Bad apedog or see why Rebel's scared?

Oh dear. Hard head stuff. Um. Bubble in my head. Pop!

Go help Rebel, he is a Junior Dog. Also, he is closer to my ape-puppies. I can always find the Bad apedog later. Rebel and I can do it together. Anyway, there is lots of scary shouting and yelling from all the apedogs on the other side of the wood.

Rabbits?

"NEENAW NEENAW."

Push off wuzzock. THIS IS THE POLICE. WE'RE COMING IN."

It's Auntie Zoo's Feathery! She's flying round and round barking.

Turn, run back. Sniff snortle, sniff snortle. Where are Rebel and his Packleader? And the Bad apedog? Find Rebel's trail, sniff snortle . . . around this bush, past these trees (quick Wet Message, hide one of Garage Dog's). Past this heap of big stones . . .

Oh. How funny. The smells of Rebel and his Packleader and the Bad apedog are there but . . .

Nobody. Just a hole in the earth under some more rocks.

Lulu sits on the rock. **"Arrk, arrk. Wuzzock, wuzzock. Bad bad."**

Smell . . . Sniff snortle . . .

Gosh. They went in the hole. Wow. Dark in there. Scary. Oh dear. Maybe very big rabbits. Or badgers. Or foxes. Or ALL OF THEM.

And a Bad Enemy apedog who might be Fierce and bite my ear.

Maybe if I bark very loudly and helpfully outside, Rebel and his Packleader will hear and come out.

RRROOOOF, ROOOF, RRRROOOOF, ARRRF, ARRRROOOOF!

Smell. Rebel's Packleader and the Enemy apedog are fighting! They are struggling! Phew. Chiff. Very very strong smell of angry mature male apedogs.

Maybe a bit too scary to go in there.

My ape-puppies are hiding in another bush, eating some ROAST BEEF. I think I'll go and . . . Oh. They finished it too quick.

Sad Dog.

ARRROOOF! ARRRF!

Here is Rebel coming out of the hole. All his fur is up, he is scared.

Hello, Rebel, what have you got there?

Hi, Jack, it is a bit too scary for me in the dark.

Well that's true. *But what about helping your Packleader fight the Bad Enemy apedog, Rebel?*

Um . . . scared puppy . . . Might bite my ear. Also, smell what I found!

Oh. A nice very MATURE BONE, long and thin. Hmm. Sniff.

Grrrr, says Rebel. He thinks I might take his bone.

All right, Friend Rebel, it's your bone. Maybe I'll go and smell if I can find a bone too.

Okay, plenty for you too, says Rebel.

Go in the hole under the rocks where Rebel found the bone.

SMELL BONE!
FOR ME!

The earth is fresh, the hole has only been here a short time. Very dark. Much apedog grunting and panting. They are wrestling. Shall I bite the Enemy apedog?

Maybe not. I don't know how. I have never ever bitten an apedog. Never bitten anybody, really. Except My Rabbit, whenever it was.

Oh dear.

Snifff sniff . . . Yes. MATURE BONES that way. Carefully go around Rebel's Packleader and the Bad apedog. Clinky stuff, sharp and breakable. Bowls and cups made of that burned earth my Packleader makes sometimes. Metal things under a rock. The kind of metal my Pack Lady wears in her ears. Smell only a bit of metal. Lots of stuff.

But also NICE MATURE BONES. Sniff sniff. Here's a big round one. MINE NOW!

Oh NO! Rebel's Packleader and the Bad apedog

have bumped into the bit of wood next to the hole where we came in.

Pitter patter ... ARRRF!
scumble thud thud.

Pitter patter
The earth FELL DOWN!

THERE IS NO HOLE.

Oh dear. Oh dear. No more air moving, smell of fresh earth. Oh dear!

Pant gasp, says Rebel's Packleader. Loud clicks. "Now STAY STILL!"

SUDDEN BRIGHT LIGHT. Makes my eyes wrinkly and sore. Blink blink. Whine. It's Rebel's Packleader with his carrying-light. He has got the Bad apedog by an arm. The Bad apedog has his clever paws held behind his back by a metal thing. He is panting and gasping too and all covered in mud. Rebel's Packleader is nicely covered too. He smells very fine.

He is THE WINNER.

143

ARRRF! I bark respectfully. You are **THE WINNER,** Rebel's Packleader. All by yourself you fought and won against another **FIERCE MALE APE– DOG.** You are very **BIG AND STRONG AND FIERCE.** Much much respect.

Rebel's Packleader has his mouth open. He is looking around with his carrying-light.

We are in a little room made of rock with swirly patterns like water on the walls. There is a rock with mature bones and metal things under it, burned-earth things around it. Where the hole was is a lot of earth and a rock fallen down. There are some Flicker Boxes and Howling and Banging boxes next to it, piled up.

"Good . . . heavens!" says Rebel's Packleader. "What the . . . ?" He points his carrying-light at the mature bones and all the other old apedog stuff. "This must be incredibly old." He sounds pleased about the mature bones too. Oh dear. I hope there will be enough.

Outside I can hear that Rebel is barking at the place where the hole isn't. He is barking loudly. He is scared. Me too. It's only a little room made of rock. How do I get out? Oh dear!

I bark too. ARRRRF ARRRF ARRRRF.

Help! PACKLEADER, QUICK. PACKMEMBERS, QUICK. ARRRF ARRRF ARROOOOF ARROOOOOO! I am a poor scared puppy dog. Get me out of this little room made of rock.... ARRROOOOOO!

Rebel's Packleader sees that the hole isn't there anymore, smells scared as well as interested.

"Rebel! You there, boy?"

Rebel barks back. ARRF WOOOOF WOOOF WOOOF.

"Watch, Rebel," shouts his Packleader. "Watch!"

Rebel barks even more helpfully. ARROOO! ARRROOO!

The Bad apedog suddenly sits down on the ground and starts doing the apedog howly thing with water in his eyes. Oh dear. Poor apedog, have you got a hurty?

Maybe I should lick you, make you feel better.

I bring the round bone over so I don't lose it. Then I go and lick the howling apedog's face, make him feel better. . . . He howls more.

It must be a bad hurty. Even though you are a Bad apedog, I will help you. Lick lick. Dribble, lick lick lick.

"Gerrimoffme!" he howls encouragingly. More licking.

"Down, Jack," says Rebel's Packleader, not very loudly or very firmly. His body says: *This is funny, I don't really mean it.*

The Bad apedog isn't happier. He is still howling. Okay. Go find my nice round bone.

"What the . . . ?" says Rebel's Packleader. "What have you got there, Jack?"

Oh, all right. Since you are Rebel's Packleader and you just won a fight with a Bad apedog. You are probably a bit hungry. You can have my bone.

Sigh.

Rebel's Packleader gets my round bone and points his shiny bright carrying-light at it. It looks a bit apedoggish but it's too old to smell what sort of animal it was.

"Holy . . . wow. Jack, do you know what you found?"

Yes, Rebel's Packleader. It is a round bone, like a ball. Can I have it back now?

Rebel's Packleader has the big eyes and mouth of a surprised apedog. The Bad apedog makes more water in his eyes. "Oh, that's horrible, is it . . . ooorgh . . . sniff."

" 'Alas, poor Yorick!' . . . I'm afraid I can't let you chew this skull, Jack. It might be evidence."

Oh, all right. You can put it up on a rock for later. Yes, there are more bones over there. You can go and smell them.

Rebel's Packleader doesn't smell them, but he puts the shiny light on them and all around them. His voice gets more and more excited. "I know what this is. This is . . . a burial chamber. Good Lord. What a find!" He turns to his beaten enemy. "You. How did you find this place?"

The Bad ape-

dog is wrinkling his face, staring at the ground. Are you feeling poorly again, Not-MyPack vanquished apedog? Let me clean your face some more. Lick. Dribble. Slurp.

"Ow ow, oooorrrggh. Gerrimoffme!" The Bad apedog is still doing howling with water, despite my helpful licking. "We didn't know about all that stuff. We thought it was just badgers . . ."

"This?"

"We were keeping . . . things in it."

"Stolen goods?"

"Yeah." The Bad apedog is just doing puppy whines now. "I'm scared. We might die. What if it all falls down?"

Rebel's Packleader looks up at the rock roof.

149

I look up, sniff sniff. There's a bit of air coming in from somewhere, but not much. Oh dear. I think that might be bad.

ARRRF ARRRF ARRRF. Rebel is still barking helpfully outside.

"You thought *badgers* did this? How big do you think they are?"

"Karl said it was just an old mine working. He said we could keep the stuff here and hide here if we had to."

"So he knew you boys were robbing the village?"

"He said all the cops would be too busy keeping him and his tree huggers away from the developers—we'd be in and out easy, like at Oldchester last month. I don't wanna die . . . !"

The apedog makes more water in his eyes. Rebel's Packleader is smelling much-thinking as well as scared.

Oh dear oh dear. My tummy is frightened. I don't like being in this funny cave even though Rebel's Packleader is with me. Sniff the rock walls. Sniff the ground. Aha! Here is his Bad Headthing.

Grrrrr . . . You Bad Headthing, you

can't sit on apedog heads and look scary,
I will get you. . . . Pounce. Bite.
"Oh no, Jack, no, not my hat!"
GRRRRRRRR. . . . Bite, chew,

SHAKE ... GRRRRRrrr.

"Oh, you idiot."
GRROWF GRRRRRR GRRROWF.
Shake shake bite,

stand
        on it,

r r r r r i p.

Good. I made it into meat. Well, not meat, maybe—sort of bits of removable fur and shoe-stuff and bits of metal. Apedog Bad Headthings are quite complicated. Interesting smell of Rebel's Packleader's hair: he washes it with stuff that smells of trees.

"You've ripped it to shreds. Why? What harm has my hat ever done you, Jack?"

It's all safe now, Rebel's Packleader, the Bad Headthing won't sit on your head and be scary any more.[1] Whew. That's better. One less thing to worry about.

I come and sit on Rebel's Packleader's feet. He pats me. Ohh ahhh . . . so nice. Paws up, you can pat my tummy. Grooooaaan. Lovely. Scratch scratch.

The Bad apedog watches. "Is he yours?"

"No, he's just a big softie, aren't you, Jack."

I still don't like it here. There aren't any more Bad Headthings to chew up, are there? Oh. Smell. Lulu is out there, going *ark ark*. I can hear her very well. Pad pad. Quick lick of the Bad apedog. Round the back of the stone with the mature bones. Oh, that's where the air is coming. Aha. A badger hole. Snifff snortle. Push my head in. That's the way out.

---

[1] The Big Yellow Stupid has always hated hats. We find they make perfectly acceptable Cat bedding if well pawed down and squashed, but otherwise they are completely pointless.

Come on, Rebel's Packleader and vanquished apedog. This way.

Rebel's Packleader looks, shakes his head. This is apedog bodytalk for: *Oh dear.*

Well, it is a bit small, but . . . Push into the hole. Push. My tummy is a bit round for it, but I can push a bit more. There is rock all around. Push. Ouch. Hurty tum. Push push, scrabble, scrape.

YES! Outside on the other side of the hump with trees in. Great! Now, where are my Packmembers?

DOUGHNUT! FOR ME! ♥

Rebel is still barking, I can hear him. But my Packmembers can't hear him because of all the apedog shouting at the edge of the wood. They are hiding in some bushes because they are scared Auntie Zoo will find them and be cross. I can smell that they are scared.

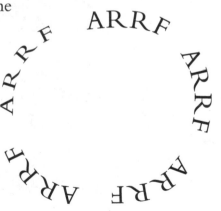

154

Run round and round barking.

Nobody can hear.

Oh dear.

RRROWF ROWF ARRRF ARROOOF. I wonder why I am barking? There is something scary about Rebel's Packleader but I can't remember what it is. Where is he? *Rebel, hi there, where is your Packleader?*

I'm not sure, I think he is eating my bones, but I have to bark now: WOOOF ARRROOOF!

Oh dear. Pad pad, run run. Back to the other place. Sniff snortle. Hi there, Rebel's Packleader. How did you get in a rabbit hole?

"Go get help, Jack," says Rebel's Packleader. "Go on. Some more stones fell down. Fetch, boy."

WHAT? There are no sticks? You have lovely mature

bones there, Rebel's Packleader, why is your tummy tense? Is it being in a dark rabbit hole?

Here is a stick for you.

"Not that. Fetch people. Get Pete and Mikey! And Auntie Zoo! Okay?"

No, Rebel's Packleader, I'm very sorry, I do not know what you want. It is making my head hurt lots, especially with all the shouting from the ape-dogs. Here is another nice stick for you to chew. There. Happy now?

"Boy, are you thick, Jack. You're even thicker than Rebel. You make him look like a genius."

Thank you, thank you, Rebel's Packleader, I am Thick. Thick is Good. I am the THICKEST DOG IN THE WORLD! Proud dog! Rebel's Packleader says I am Thick. Thicker than Rebel.

PROUD DOG! ARRRF. ARRRF.

I am Hungry. Oh look. A van. It's a different van, not the same smell as the one the Bad apedogs were in. I wonder where the Food is. . . .

Sniff snortle, snifff . . .

Yes! The window is open! Yes! I can get through, even with my round tummy, if I hup and kick and scrabble with my back legs. OOooff.

Yum. The food is there, but where? It is a dough-nut. I know it is. Yum yum! I like doughnuts!

Sniff snortle, sniff. Smell the seats. Smell under the seats. Apedog stuff—I don't like apple cores. Where is my doughnut? Snnnnnifffff.

It's near here. Where the interesting sticks and the big round thing for holding are. Better be a bit careful. Bad things happen where there are big round things and interesting sticks. Not sure what, but Bad.

Doughnut?

Sniffff . . . Aha. I found it. It's on the little shelf there. Get it with my nose. Sniff. Yum. I like dough-nut. Sit on the seat, put my paws on the round thing, put my nose where the doughnut is stuck.

BEEEEP!

What?

Try again.

BEEEEP!

BEEEEP!

BEEEEEEEEEEEEP!

Why is the van barking? There are no Enemy dogs. It is hard to get my doughnut. I have to lean my tummy on the round thing and push with my nose and lick lick lick . . .

BEEEEP!

BEEEEEEEEEEEEEEEEEEEE
EEEEEEEEEEEEEEEEEP!

Yes! Got it! Yum yum snortle gulp erp.

Maybe sleep now on a comfy seat?

DIG! DIG!

"Jack! What are you doing in there?"

It's Caroline and Mikey and Pete. My Pack-members.

Well, you can't have my doughnut, Pack-members, sorry, but it's mine. Slurp, lick, gulp.
Never mind the paper, eat all of it. Yum yum. I like doughnuts even if they make my teeth feel funny.

ARRRF. Poke my head out of the window.

They open the back and I get out easier. My poor tummy is a bit sore and very covered in mud.

"Where's Rebel and Officer Janner? What happened to your tummy?"

Who? Oh, I know where Rebel is. Can't you hear him barking? He is puzzled and scared because he has lost his Packleader.

Something about Rebel's Packleader is worrying me, but I don't know what. Let's go home? Oh Okay, put my leash on. Here's Rebel.

wooof WOOF, WOOF.

Hi, Rebel, nice to smell you.

Hi, Jack, but this is my bone, you can't have my bone.

Oh yes, I remember now. There are good bones in this rabbit hole. Come on, Pete, I'll show you some lovely mature bones. Yum. Here is the rabbit hole where the rocks are. Smell. Lovely mature bones and . . .

Rebel's Packleader! And the Bad apedog!

ARROOOOF! Hi, Rebel's Packleader, how lovely to smell you again!

"Help!" shouts Rebel's Packleader. "Can you hear us!"

"Help!" shouts the Bad apedog.

Caroline and Pete look around to find where

the shouting is from. They look up in the trees.

Mikey goes to the rabbit hole and leans in. "Are you rabbits?" he asks.

"Hi there, Mikey," says Rebel's Packleader. "Can you get your auntie?"

"Are you stuck like Winnie the Pooh?"

"Yes."

"Oh wow," shouts Pete. "Look, it's Officer Janner and somebody else. Look. They're down there. How did you get there?"

"Long story, Pete. Can you get help? We can't get out and I'm worried the roof is unstable."

"Oh wow. Right. Okay. Right."

"Go get your Auntie Zoo."

"Er . . . but . . . um . . . well, Okay."

Pete and Caroline look at each other and at Mikey. They look over where the shouting and RRRRR things are.

"Auntie Zoo will flip out if she sees me," says Pete.

"So will my mom," says Caroline.

"How about if I say Jack got away and came here."

"Hm. We've got to tell her something."

"Oh dear."

ARRRF. I can smell that Rebel's Packleader is getting frightened. Some bits of earth fell down in the rabbit hole. He is scared in case the rocks fall down. "Kids, can you get a move on?"

ARRRF ARRRF ARRRF. I will bark at the Bad rabbit hole. ARRROOOOFF!

"I will stay here and look after Jack," says Mikey. "You and Caroline can tell Auntie Zoo."

Caroline and Pete look at each other. They hold hands. Off they go to where the apedogs are shouting.

ARROOOF! Bad rabbit hole, let Rebel's Packleader come out. ARROOOO ARROO–

OOO, YIP YIP ARRROO-OOOOO!

"I told you to go straight home, no detours, and you come straight back here and you bring Mikey as well. . . . I told you this is no place for kids and you ignored me. . . . When your mom and dad get home . . ."

It's Auntie Zoo! ARRRF ARRF ARROOO ARRROOOOOF.

"Help!" shout Rebel's Packleader and the Bad apedog. "Get us out of here!"

Auntie Zoo is too busy being cross to hear them, and Pete can't get a word in either.

A R R R F A R R R F ARROOF.

"And you brought Jack back with you as well when you know . . . ?"

ARRRF! Stop barking at the ape-puppies, and

smell! I get her removable fur very softly in my teeth and pull her to where the rabbit hole is.

"Jack, stoppit, I can see there's a rabbit hole and I'm really not interested in ..."

"HELP!" shout Rebel's Pack-leader and the Bad apedog together.

"What?" Auntie Zoo looks all over.

Pitter patter, more earth. Rebel's Packleader very scared now. "Can you hear me! I'm down here!"

At last she smells him. Why are apedogs so slow?[1] "Good lord, Officer Janner. What are you doing down there?"

"Hoping I don't get buried alive."

ARRRF ARRRF.

"How did you ...?"

"This is some kind of old burial chamber, but the entrance has fallen in. We need digging out. Quickly."

"Who's with you?"

"Huh, him," says Caroline. "That's one of Karl's mates."

---

[1] A fascinating question to which there is no easy answer.

Lots of quick ape-barking. Auntie Zoo runs off. I can see her going to where all the apedogs are shouting at each other. She pushes to the front. She shouts at everybody.

Then Lulu flies over to her, barking and shouting ape-barking.

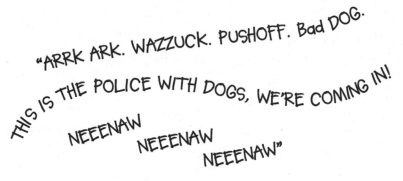

"ARRK ARK. WAZZUCK. PUSHOFF. Bad DOG. THIS IS THE POLICE WITH DOGS, WE'RE COMING IN! NEEENAW NEEENAW NEEENAW"

Lots of things happen. Very complicated to smell and hear. The young male apedog Pack suddenly stop pushing and shoving and shouting. They stop wanting to fight. The apedogs with RRRRR things stop wanting to fight. The apedogs with dark removable furs and Bad Headthings stop wanting to fight. They all turn and listen to Auntie Zoo.

More barking between them. She waves her arms. Suddenly, everything changes.

Soon lots of apedogs are here, being a quick Pack. They bark at each other. Some of them were miners once. They all talk very quick, too quick and too complicated to understand. They push a bit of pipe down through the earth so more air goes in. They dig with digging sticks. The apedogs with RRRR things get a Big Huge Kennel-that-moves with big knobbly wheels, very scary.

Rebel is scared, barks and barks, ARRRRF ARRRF GRR-RROOOOF.

 One of the officer apedogs with a Bad Head-thing comes along. His body says he is important, like a Packleader. He goes to Rebel and tries to get his collar.

Rebel thinks he is trying to get his nice mature bone. Rebel growls at him, *Stay away, mine now.*

The officer Packleader doesn't understand. He doesn't even have dog smell on his removable furs. He smells important and he thinks Rebel will know it. "Come on," he says. "Leave it, boy. Come this way."

Rebel doesn't want to leave the earthy bit where his Packleader went in. GRRRRRR, he says. *I don't like you, you can't have my bone, you can't go near my Packleader. . . .*
GRRRRRR . . .

Oh dear. Rebel is going to fight the officer apedog. Oh no. He jumps up, showing teeth, and when the officer apedog turns to run away, he BITES HIS TAIL END! Wow!

Mikey laughs lots. The officer apedog falls over and bumps himself. He is barking lots. ARRRF.

He leaves Rebel alone now. That would be best. Nobody is happy when his Packleader is lost. Also, Rebel has a bone.

Now the apedogs with digging sticks are digging

hard. They are digging out the earthy bit. They use some of the stones lying around to hold it up. Some of them have bits of flat wood ready.

ARRRF! That's right, dig that way. Lots of nice mature bones there.

Oh, and Rebel's Packleader and the Bad apedog. Probably they have chewed up the nice bones by now, what with being nervous and having whirly tummies from being stuck in a rabbit hole.

The apedogs who carry boxes and furry sticks around are here and pointing their boxes at the apedogs who are digging. Mikey is with Pete and Caroline talking to the apedog who is holding a sort of stick with a fat bit on top. Is it a chewy thing?

Hi there, are you a Friend? You smell nice, you have eaten lots of fish. Can I smell your . . . ?

Sorry.

"This is Jack, my dog," says Pete. "He's really cool. He told us where Officer Janner was. He made the horn on the van beep so we could hear, and he barked at the hole. He's a hero!"

The apedogs point their boxes at me. Oh dear. They have a long furry thing on a stick. What is it? It must be a chewy thing. Why is it on a stick?

ARRRF ARRRF ARRRF!
Jump up. Bite. Crunch. Bite,
SHAKE. It falls to bits.

The apedogs are all barking at me now. Pete and Mikey and Caroline are giggling because I ate the sound-boom. What is a "sound-boom"?

It doesn't taste very nice.

ARRRRRRF!

The Huge Kennel-that-moves with big wheels has got a rope on, going to the rock that fell down.

Now it goes backward. Pull pull . . . Dig dig. Lots of hard work. The apedogs are digging as if they are all in one Pack.

Only Auntie Zoo's ape-puppy isn't there. Karl has gone away now. When everybody else was busy digging for the mature bones, and Rebel's Pack-leader and the Bad apedog, he ran very quickly, very quietly, and got in the van where my dough-nut was, and he drove away with the other Bad apedog I had to stop chasing. I wonder why.

The apedogs with boxes bark excitedly at the boxes. Rebel barks back at them. We both bark. We are A PACK. We have little slitty eyes. GRRRR, we

don't like you apedogs with chewy furry things on sticks. . . .

All the apedogs bark very excitedly. They are helping Rebel's Packleader and the Bad apedog out of the hole they made, all barking at each other at once. The apedogs with boxes stop barking at me and Rebel and point their boxes at the hole where they can see the rocks and the mature bones.

No, you can't have those bones, those are MY BONES and REBEL'S BONES, YOU CAN'T HAVE THEM. GRRRRRRR.

Here comes Rebel's Packleader and the Bad apedog, all covered with interesting-smelling mud and smelling very happy and relieved.

Rebel jumps up and puppy-bounces, he is VERY VERY HAPPY. SO HAPPY.

I am happy too, Rebel! HAPPY HAPPY HAPPY Dog.

Rebel and his Packleader do big cuddles while the apedogs with whirring boxes and lightning boxes point at him and bark. His Packleader talks to the officer apedog that Rebel bit. He sounds a bit sad. Rebel growls at the officer apedog again.

"That's enough, Rebel. You've done it now," says Rebel's Packleader. "Why on earth did you bite the chief inspector?"

GRRRRRRR, says Rebel. *I still don't like him.*

"I'm very sorry about that, sir. I think he was frightened and upset about me being in that old burial chamber," says Rebel's Packleader. His voice is paws-up for a Senior apedog Packleader but also trying not to laugh.

Then Rebel's Packleader pats me and says I am a Good Dog. Rebel whines a little bit, but then he comes over and we do Wet Messages to show respect.

Pete and Mikey and Caroline are cuddling me now while the apedogs with boxes talk. Ohhhh ahhhh groan . . . lovely. I like this. It's great to have so much cuddling. Pat pat pat.

Happy ♥ Dog. ♥

Paws up, pat tummy. Lots of lightning boxes. Lots of apedogs talking. The people with the lightning boxes and whirring boxes on shoulders want me to sit next to Rebel's Packleader. Everybody is too excited to do any more angry barking or fighting and anyway, nobody can find Karl or his pack of young male apedogs. They have all gone away.

Auntie Zoo is sad about that, but she isn't saying anything. Lulu sits on her shoulder saying **"NEENAW"** sometimes.

All the apedogs from the soft dens are there, cheering and waving their arms, Pat pat pat the dog, me! Happy Dog.

Rebel's Packleader says to the Pack Lady with the fat furry stick: "Police Dog Rebel tracked the burglar and found the entrance to the place where they were going to hide their stolen goods—down there in the burial chamber. I think they must have found the place  when they were digging a tunnel. I made the arrest. Jack came in to keep me company. Then, when the tunnel collapsed, Jack got out through that little hole there to get help. He fetched Caroline Burley and Pete and Mikey Stopes, and

173

they acted very sensibly and fetched their aunt, who organized the rescue. Nobody could hear Rebel barking because of all the shouting. It was Jack who raised the alarm by honking the horn of the escape van."

Oh. Did I?

Is that "Good Dog"?

STEAK?

I GET STEAK!

The Cats said I should jump over a suppertime and a sleeptime.

In the night I heard Auntie Zoo talking on the talkbone. Her voice was angry and sad. "Never mind how I know. I know what you were up to with those thieves and your nasty friends."

Then I could hear her ape-puppy Karl in the talkbone. He was making whining paws-up voice for her, but she interrupted. "I'm so ashamed of you, Karl. How could you use people like that?"

Next he was barking. I came and leaned on her and growled a little, so she knew I was On Her

Side. She patted me sadly. "I know a lot of people. Either you give yourself up to the police or I'll tell everyone I can what your game is, which will put a stop to it because you won't be welcome at any protest site. Understand? No, I won't inform on you. You have to do it."

More barking from Karl. Grrrr. You are bad to your Pack Lady. You should have more respect. GRRRRR.

"Good-bye, Karl," says Auntie Zoo, and puts the talkbone back softly. She smells terribly sad. Poor poor Pack Lady. Let me lick your face, there there, cuddle.

I have a lovely sleep on her bed until she pushes me out in the middle of the night because she says I am too loud.

How am I loud? I don't think I'm loud even when I'm chasing exciting rabbits in the sleepy place.

More jumping over: breakfast time and a lovely bus ride, Walkies and coming back on the bus (CHIPS!), and spending the day doing bark- ing games with Lulu.

"ARRF ARRF," she says, sitting in her cage. **"ARRF ARRRF ARRROOOF!"**

"ARRF ARRF ARRRF ARRRRRF," I bark back. She is doing dog-barking![1] It's great. She is my Friend. Auntie Zoo has a headache. A NotMy-Pack apedog Friend Pack Lady brought back Pete and Mikey and she gave me big patting and cuddles too because I saved Pencerriog Wood. Is that a Good Dog? Oh great. Steak?

Oh. Auntie Zoo talked to the talkbone for a long time when we got home. She still sounded

---

[1] Horrible abomination! Outrageous wicked evil terrible anti-Cat behavior! How can We hunt and kill the Flying Feathery Food when it barks like a dog so We have to run away? We are actively researching better apecat lairs where Cats are decently treated.

upset and sad. I could hear my Packleader in the talkbone.

ARRF ARRF! I said. ARROOOF. Pant pant. *Hi, Great Packleader, how lovely to hear you, where are you? Can I cuddle . . . ?*

Oh. Sad Puppy. Where is he?

It's funny when apedogs are in the talkbone. You can hear them but you can't see them and you can't smell them.[2]

Auntie Zoo said what happened and did paws-up voice for my Pack Lady. Pack Lady was only a little bit mad about it. She laughed lots in the talk-bone when Auntie Zoo explained about me making the van bark and said she was sure Food was involved somehow.

Now Pete and Mikey are jumping up and down because they are going to be on the television. A TV person came to school today and talked to them about finding the Iron Age site in Pencerriog Wood. They are Famous and I am too.

What is "television"? What is "famous"?

Terri is in her room listening to her Howling and Banging box. She is very mad that she

---

2 Feline primatologists are working hard on the telephone problem. Apecats use them all the time, and it's true that they are not edible. If you knock one over, it makes pleasant purring sounds until an apecat starts to speak and then there is a nasty wailing noise. We have decided to ignore them mercilessly until they become more Cat-friendly.

wasn't there when Rebel and I found the mature bones and isn't going to be on the TV.

Where is my STEAK? No steak. Sigh. Doze.

What's that? I can hear happy-footsteps. Pack-leader is back! Pack Lady is back! Here they are, coming through the door.

OH HAPPY HAPPY HAPPY JOYFUL HAPPY DOG!!!★★★Wag

Hi, arrrf arrrf . . . Jump, hop, dance dance. Puppy dance! You have been GONE FOR SO LONG!

Did you get any GOOD FOOD? Where is my STEAK? Snifff. Something nice in Packleader's bag. Mmm.

HAPPY HAPPY. Puppy-bow, Wag wag, ARRRF ARRRF ARRF ARRF, Packleader, welcome, Pack Lady, can I smell your . . . ?

Sorry.

Pat pat. Can I have Food now, Great Packleader?

Okay, the puppies can have a cuddle.

The Flicker Box is on. Pete and Mikey are pointing at bits in it. Terri is watching too; her body says: *Huh, unfair.*

There is barking.

GREAT! I can hear my friend Rebel. ARRRRF! *Hi, Rebel, come in!*

How funny. I can hear him in the Flicker Box, but I can't smell him. Another dog is barking. Oh dear. He sounds Big and Loud and Scary.

ARRROOOF. ARRROOOF. ARR–ROOF.

Lots of ape-barking and laughing. Some NotMy-Pack apedog Friends have come. They are all talking at once and drinking Falling Over Juice made from bad grapes. Trot out to the hall, sniff snortle snifff snortle. Removable-fur boxes. Hm. No one there. Lurk. Pull. Yum yum.

"Pencerriog Wood might be one of the most important Iron Age sites in the West Country," says Packleader. "I was talking to one of the archaeology experts at the Inquiry and he said that there's no way they'll build a road there now, not when they've got real burial chambers to investigate and all the art-ifacts to study. Some of the ceramics were damaged and they think a fox or even a wolf might have had a go at some of the bones, but . . ."

They all cheer and point at the Flicker Box.

More dog-barking. Maybe he isn't so Big and Scary. He sounds a bit familiar. All the apedogs say, "Wahoo," and I am getting lots of pats and cuddles.

Pack Lady is talking to another Pack Lady.

"They'll probably build over the old Second World War aerodrome, which is where they were supposed to do it in the first place," says Pack Lady. "It's the obvious sensible route. And it's all thanks to Jack. Ooops. I nearly forgot! Where's Jack's present, Tom?"

"It's in my bag."

Pack Lady goes and looks. Um.

Oh dear.

Maybe this is Bad Dog. It was a very delicious-smelling Steak, Pack Lady, and there was a little teeny hole in the bag and I couldn't help it . . .

"JACK! YOU GREEDY PIG!"

Oh dear.

"It's all right," says Packleader, coming out with more Falling Over Juice for Pack Lady. "It was his steak in the first . . . OH JACK! YOU GREEDY PIG!"

"Belgian chocolates!" wails Pack Lady in a terribly sad voice.

Yes, Pack Lady. I like chocolate too.

And STEAK. I love STEAK. MORE?

ERP.

Jackspeak: English

B

Bad Headthing	hat
between-ears face	forehead
Big Furry-with-hard-clip-clop paws	horse
Big Hunt	supermarket shopping
Big White Water Dish	toilet
brown tails	dreadlocks
burned earth	ceramic

C

Cats' God	fire
carblood	oil
carjuice	gasoline
carry-boxes	suitcases
carrying-light	flashlight
claw-smearing	nail polishing
clicky-clacky Flicker Box	computer
Cold Cupboard	fridge
colored paper	money

D

Den	where Jack lives, house
Den That Moves	moving van/bus
digging stick	spade

F

Falling Over Juice	wine
fat stick	microphone
flappy things on sticks	placards
Flicker Box	television
Flying Featheries	birds
food-skin	packaging
Funny Pricklies	hedgehogs

G

ground-with-NotGrass	flowerbed

H

Hard Message	poo
hard-shelled food	can
hot brown drink	coffee
Howling and Banging box	portable stereo
Huge Great Food Place	superstore

I

interesting sticks	gearshift and hand brake

K

Kennel That Moves	car

L

leg-coverings	trousers
lightning box	camera
light-tree	lamppost

Little Crawlies	insects
Lots of Dens Together place	town

M

making into meat	killing
meat-skin	package
Medium Eatable Furries with Long Ears	rabbits
message huts	portable toilets
mouth-happy-squeaky-thing	squeaky plastic hedgehog toy

N

NEEEOOWWW things	jet planes
nest	bed
nest-coverings	bedspreads
NotFetch	you fetch the stick and then forget to bring it back

O

Outside	yard
Outside Outside	everywhere else

P

pawball	good game involving ape-puppies kicking

	a ball, Jack pawing it, and then Jack biting it until it turns into a rag
paw-coverings	shoes/boots/socks
piled-up bread	sandwich
plastic biscuit	bank card
prechewed cow-meat	ground beef

R	Ready	in season
	removable furs	clothes
	roaring-sucky-tube	vacuum cleaner
	round thing	steering wheel
	round tick-tick thing	clock
	RRRR-thing	chainsaw (any mechanical cutter)

S	shoe stuff	leather
	singed bread	toast
	Slimys	frogs
	Small Fierce Brown Wild Dog	fox
	Smaller Fierce Stripy Face	badger
	Small Furries	mice, voles, hamsters, etc.
	Smoke Message	exhaust fumes

smoky-sticks	cigarettes
snail-trail stick	pen
soft apedog dens	tents
soft paper with ink smudges	newspapers
Special	pregnant
Special Messages	puppies

T

tail end	bottom
talkbone	telephone
things-that-look-like-sausages-but-made-of-plant	vegetarian sausages
two-wheel-go-fast thing	bike

U

unswallow	vomit

W

water-howling	crying
Water NotFurries	fish
water-running	swimming
weeaweeaw cars	police cars/ambulance
Wet Message	pee
Whitecoat apedog	vet

ABOUT THE AUTHOR

Jack Perry was born near Plymouth on April 7, 1993, the only pup in his litter. After a brief time with someone else, he was adopted (at great expense) by the Perry Pack and their Owner, Remy.[1] Jack has moved dens twice and went to obedience school in Camborne, where he was not at all obedient and far too friendly. His interests include eating, walking, food, swimming, breakfast, playing pawball with his Pack, supper, playing NotFetch and, of course, food theft. He is an accomplished cereal killer, dustbin desperado, and birthday-cake bandit. Apart from this, however, he is mostly a Good Dog and is very gentle with everyone.

Since *I, Jack* was published, Jack has become an

---

[1] Nobody asked ME.

accomplished Media Dog. He has pawed books in bookshops, had his picture in the local newspaper, and given barks to primary school children. Pack Lady comes along to interpret and is often quite mean with the dog-biscuit royalties. Jack is available[2] for author appearances so long as he doesn't have to travel too far and is provided with a bowl of water and some Outside for Wet Messages.

---

[2] We, however, do not stoop to such vulgar crowd-pleasing and would in any case be extremely expensive.

Patricia Finney is Jack's real Pack Lady. She spends a lot of time running around after Jack, the Cats, her three children, and the Packleader. When she can, she writes all kinds of things, including historical and contemporary novels, scripts, and articles for newspapers (winning the David Higham Award for her first novel), despite the Cats' constant attempts to stop her by marching across the clicky-clacky Flicker Box's keyboard and making it

crash

hhhh<>%^$£*&^

hhhh<>%^$£*&^